***Jesse couldn't stop staring at Hannah. She was the most wonderful woman he'd ever met. She deserved everything in the world.***

But he wasn't certain he could give her anything.

He didn't know if he had anything to give.

To her. To the Ryans. To anyone.

He'd promised himself he'd stay emotionally detached—uninvolved until he sorted out his memories and had time to figure things out.

He glanced at Hannah again. How on earth could he sort anything out when all he could do was think about her? And how much he wanted—needed—her?

She deserved a man who was permanent, a husband who'd give her all that she wanted, needed and deserved. And a man who could be a father to her daughter, Riley. A real father, one who could love openly with no hesitation.

How could Jesse give Hannah or Riley any part of himself when he still didn't know who he was?

Dear Reader,

This May, we celebrate Mother's Day and a fabulous month of uplifting romances. I'm delighted to introduce RITA® Award finalist Carol Stephenson, who debuts with her heartwarming reunion romance, *Nora's Pride*. Carol writes, "*Nora's Pride* is very meaningful to me, as my mother, my staunchest fan and supporter, passed away in May 2000. I'm sure she's smiling down at me from heaven. She passionately believed this would be my first sale." A must-read for your list!

*The Princess and the Duke*, by Allison Leigh, is the second book in the CROWN AND GLORY series. Here, a princess and a duke share a kiss, but can their love withstand the truth about a royal assassination? We have another heart-thumper from the incomparable Marie Ferrarella with *Lily and the Lawman*, a darling city-girl-meets-small-town-boy romance.

In *A Baby for Emily*, Ginna Gray delivers an emotionally charged love story in which a brooding hero lays claim to a penniless widow who, unbeknownst to her, is carrying *their* child.... Sharon De Vita pulls on the heartstrings with *A Family To Come Home To*, in which a rugged rancher searches for his family and finds true love! You also won't want to miss Patricia McLinn's *The Runaway Bride*, a humorous tale of a sexy cowboy who rescues a distressed bride.

I hope you enjoy these exciting books from Silhouette Special Edition—the place for love, life and family. Come back for more winning reading next month!

Sincerely,

Karen Taylor Richman
Senior Editor

# A Family To Come Home To

## SHARON DE VITA

Silhouette®

SPECIAL EDITION™

Published by Silhouette Books
America's Publisher of Contemporary Romance

This book is dedicated with sincere awe, appreciation and thanks to the incredibly courageous men and women of the New York Fire and Police Departments who truly define the word *heroes*. And to everyone who has ever worn the uniform of our great country, including my own husband, Colonel Frank Noland Cushing (Ret), for not just defending our country and our freedoms, but for having the courage to stand tall in the face of evil and never waver no matter what the odds. We are awed by your courage, proud of your accomplishments and eternally thankful for your commitment.

SILHOUETTE BOOKS

ISBN 0-373-24468-1

A FAMILY TO COME HOME TO



This edition published by arrangement with Harlequin Books S.A.



Visit Silhouette at www.eHarlequin.com

**Printed in U.S.A.**

**Books by Sharon De Vita**

Silhouette Special Edition

*Child of Midnight* #1013
**The Lone Ranger* #1078
**The Lady and the Sheriff* #1103
**All It Takes Is Family* #1126
†*The Marriage Basket* #1307
†*The Marriage Promise* #1313
††*With Family in Mind* #1450
††*A Family To Come Home To* #1468

Silhouette Books

The Coltons
*I Married a Sheik*

Silhouette Romance

*Heavenly Match* #475
*Lady and the Legend* #498
*Kane and Mabel* #545
*Baby Makes Three* #573
*Sherlock's Home* #593
*Italian Knights* #610
*Sweet Adeline* #693
****On Baby Patrol** #1276
****Baby with a Badge** #1298
****Baby and the Officer** #1316
†*The Marriage Badge* #1443
††*Anything for Her Family* #1580
††*A Family To Be* #1586

*Silver Creek County
†The Blackwell Brothers
††Saddle Falls
**Lullabies and Love

---

## *SHARON DE VITA,*

a former adjunct professor of literature and communications, is a *USA Today* bestselling, award-winning author of numerous works of fiction and nonfiction. Her first novel won a national writing competition for Best Unpublished Romance Novel of 1985. This award-winning book, *Heavenly Match*, was subsequently published by Silhouette in 1985. Sharon has over two million copies of her novels in print, and her professional credentials have earned her a place in *Who's Who in American Authors, Editors and Poets* as well as the *International Who's Who of Authors*. In 1987, Sharon was the proud recipient of the *Romantic Times* Lifetime Achievement Award for Excellence in Writing.

A newlywed, Sharon met her husband while doing research for one of her books. The widowed, recently retired military officer was so wonderful, Sharon decided to marry him after she interviewed him! Sharon and her new husband have seven grown children, five grandchildren, and currently reside in Arizona.

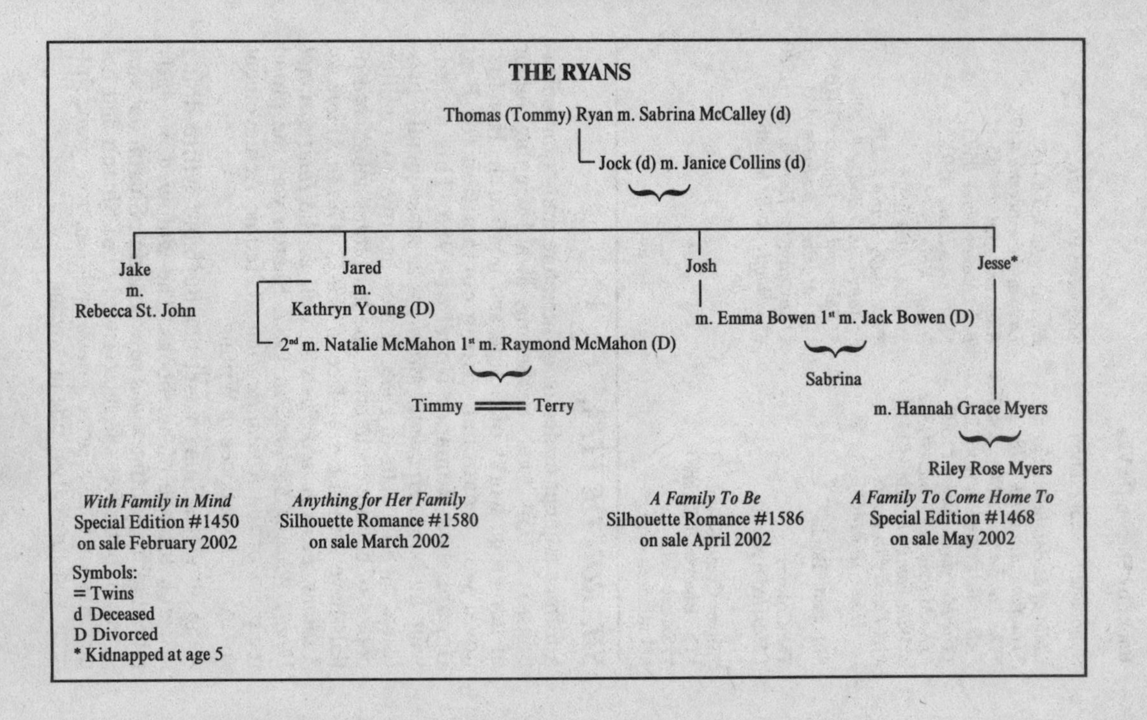
THE RYANS
Thomas (Tommy) Ryan m. Sabrina McCalley (d)
Jock (d) m. Janice Collins (d)
Jake
m.
Rebecca St. John
Jared
m.
Kathryn Young (D)
2nd m. Natalie McMahon 1st m. Raymond McMahon (D)
Timmy = Terry
Josh
m. Emma Bowen 1st m. Jack Bowen (D)
Sabrina
Jesse*
m. Hannah Grace Myers
Riley Rose Myers
With Family in Mind
Special Edition #1450
on sale February 2002
Anything for Her Family
Silhouette Romance #1580
on sale March 2002
A Family To Be
Silhouette Romance #1586
on sale April 2002
A Family To Come Home To
Special Edition #1468
on sale May 2002
Symbols:
= Twins
d Deceased
D Divorced
* Kidnapped at age 5

## *Prologue*

*Southwind Community Hospital*
*Southwind, Texas*

Time was running out.

Grace Garland knew that in these last few moments of life she had to make right a wrong or she'd never have any peace.

With her eyes glazed with pain, she licked her lips and lovingly looked at her son.

*Her son.*

He'd always been her pride and joy. Her sole reason for living. It hadn't been easy being a woman alone raising a child, but she'd always felt he was her very own miracle.

Oh, how she'd loved him, nurtured him, guided him.

*And lied to him.*

"J-Jesse?" Lifting a trembling hand, she touched his face. A face she'd loved from the moment she'd laid eyes on it so many years ago.

"Mama." His smile was gentle. "It's all right, Ma. I'm here." The deep timbre of his voice was shaky with grief. "Rest now, Ma, save your strength."

"No. Jesse, son, there's something I...have to... tell...you."

Rocked by unbearable pain, her eyes slid closed and the memories came again. Fractured, disjointed, but so very vivid and real. With some effort, she remembered the day he'd come to her.

Just a small boy, terribly frightened, terribly alone. He was only five, but his glorious blue eyes were haunted by some fear she could only imagine.

*Her son.*

She had to tell him the truth. Had to tell him she'd lied to him; a lie that had haunted her for almost twenty years.

"Jesse." Forcing her eyes open again, she struggled to focus on him. He was a man now. A strong, fine man. Even grown, he remained a loner who had never quite come out of his shell, at least not with others.

Whatever had happened to him before he'd come to her, he'd never spoken of it. She wasn't even sure he remembered it. At the time it didn't seem important. Now it was the most important thing in the world.

"Jesse." She whispered his name again. It was getting harder to breathe, the pain was creeping closer. "I have to tell you something, son."

Tenderly, he stroked the hair from her dampened forehead. "Don't try to talk, Ma. Just rest. It can wait."

''No.'' The word croaked out and she reached for his hand, held on like a lifeline. The pain was stealing over her body, sapping the little bit of strength she had left. ''I...I have to tell you now, before it's too late.''

''Ma, please, don't talk like that.'' Panic ripped through him; he was losing her. She was his mother, the only family he'd ever known. And now she was dying and there was nothing he could do about it.

''Jesse, I love you more than anything in the world—'' She had to swallow. ''But, Jesse, you're not my son. You were stolen as a child.''

Pain sliced through her, cutting off her breath. A whimper escaped and her eyes slid closed, but she knew she had to go on, to do this final act of love. For him. Always for him.

''What?'' Panicked and confused, Jesse almost dismissed her words as ramblings brought on by the enormous amount of pain and medication. But her eyes fluttered open and for a brief moment they were clear and bright as they met his, and he knew in that instant she was telling him the truth.

A terrible fear like a living thing sprang up, encompassing his whole being, shaking the foundation of everything he believed. He wanted to tell her to stop, that it didn't matter, wasn't important. But he couldn't.

''W-what are you talking about, Ma?'' His gaze searched her face. ''Mama?''

''Jesse, twenty years ago my half brother, Charlie...Lord, I loved him, but he was always in trouble. Well, he got himself into some real serious financial trouble. His wealthy wife was divorcing him, and he owed money to some very bad people. Charlie, he always had some get-rich-quick scheme, but this time he outdid himself.''

Jesse struggled to contain the emotions churning through him. ''What did he do?''

Grace had to fight for breath through the ever-increasing pain. ''He had this idea, supposedly harmless, he said, but it would solve all his financial problems. He was going to kidnap one of the sons of some very prominent family, hold him for a few days until the family paid the ransom, then return the kid to his family.''

The fear grew, snaking along Jesse's skin like a virulent virus, covering every inch of his mind, his emotions. ''What…what happened?''

''Something went wrong. Apparently one of the ladies Charlie had been seeing took it upon herself to write a ransom note as well, so Charlie knew he'd never get any money out of the family.'' Her breath came out in short, jerky gasps, but she was determined to continue. ''Charlie was terrified because he had this kid he didn't know what to do with, and he was frantic that the authorities might be on to him and the people he owed money were looking for him. He knew he had to disappear until things cooled off, but he didn't know what to do with the little boy.'' Grace squeezed Jesse's hand, drawing it to her cheek to feel his warmth one last time.

He didn't want to ask, didn't want to know, even though deep in the recesses of his heart he suddenly knew. And it brought on a wave of sadness and grief he'd never known existed before.

"Mama...the little boy...what did...Charlie do with the little boy?"

She hesitated for a long moment, her eyes fluttering closed before finally opening again. She took a long, labored breath that slowly wheezed out of her.

Panicked, Jesse's gaze shifted to the machines next to the bed monitoring her vital signs. They were weak and shaky. The familiar beep of the heart monitor grew weaker, slower.

"Mama?" He waited until she'd gathered enough strength to speak.

"He brought that boy to me, Jesse. Charlie always knew how badly I wanted babies. I'd never made a secret of it, but an infection in my teens ruined any chance I had of giving birth. It was a heartbreak I almost couldn't bear. So when Charlie asked me to take care of the little boy for a while..." Her voice trailed off and she met his gaze again. "I couldn't refuse." She paused. "Jesse, that boy was...you."

He stared at her in disbelief for a moment, a torrent of emotions shocking, then rocking him.

"Oh God." Jesse lowered his head, fought back the grief and all the other emotions that were so strong he felt as if he was choking on them.

"I'm sorry I lied to you, son. But I fell in love with you right from the start. You were just a little bitty thing back then, barely five and scared to death. You didn't speak for almost a year."

He hadn't spoken for a year? Feeling desperate, and slightly sick, Jesse forced himself to concentrate on the myriad questions that suddenly had no answers. "Ma, what...what happened to Charlie?"

She hesitated, then said, "Don't rightly know. I never heard from him again. I reckon he might have been killed or something, otherwise I would have heard from him for sure."

"He just took off and left me with you?" Jesse couldn't hide the horror in his voice, his heart.

"Guess he didn't know what else to do. He never told me who you really were, and I didn't want to know, because then I figured I would have had to honor my Christian duty and return you to your family—your real family, and Jesse, honey, I couldn't bear to do that. I simply couldn't." Tears spilled down her cheeks and she paused to try to get her breath. "Oh, I thought about turning you over to the authorities, but truth be told, I loved you so much by then I was so afraid of losing you. Afraid too, if I called the authorities, I'd go to jail as well for helping Charlie. I was young, son, and scared, and all I knew was that I finally had what I'd always wanted all along—a child. So...I did the only thing I could, the only thing I knew how to do. I kept my mouth shut, and considered myself blessed. I raised you as my own, honey. But I loved you so by then, son. In my heart, you *were* my son."

*Son.*

Jesse's head jerked up. *He wasn't her son.* Had never been her son. He'd been born to someone else, another family. A family he'd been stolen from so many years ago.

*Who the hell was he?*

The distress on his face frightened Grace in a way nothing had in a long time.

"Jesse, please try to understand. I did what I thought

was best—'' Pain sliced through her, cutting off her words and her eyes slid closed to try to block out the pain. Tears warmed her cheeks as she tried to continue, knowing the truth could cost her the only thing that had ever mattered to her.

''Mama? Ma!'' With his thumb, Jesse tenderly wiped her tears, feeling his own throat burn and his own eyes grow moist. He was losing her in so many ways, and he didn't know if he could handle any of them. ''Mama, please, can you hear me? Talk to me, please!''

Her eyes fluttered open. Grace struggled to get Jesse in focus. The pain was too strong now, hazing her vision, blurring her thoughts. She clung to his hand, not wanting to let go, not wanting to lose him, not now.

''I'm dying, Jesse—''

''No, no, don't say that.'' Raw panic grabbed him. ''Don't say that, Ma.''

''Hush, now, son, I'm dying and there's no denying it.'' She hesitated, then tried to smile, all the while trying to get some air into her aching lungs. ''I want you to do something for me, Jesse. Please? Do this one last thing for me?''

He hunched forward in the chair in order to hear her. ''What, Ma, what? Anything. I'll do anything you ask. You know that.'' He always had; he always would. She was his mother. Nothing—nothing would change that.

''All these years...I've worried about your kin, wondered about them. I can't imagine what they must have gone through losing you like that.'' She clung to his hand. ''I'm so sorry for what I did to them. And to you, Jesse, especially to you.''

He couldn't ever remember crying, but he felt hot tears sting the back of his eyes now. "Ma—"

"No, Jesse, listen to me." With a strength that surprised him, she squeezed his hand. "I want you to find your family, Jesse, do you hear me? Find your real kin. Find them so they can finally have some peace. It's time, Jesse, time for you to go home."

*Home?*

He thought he was home; thought *she* was his home.

"Ma, I don't even know—" He dragged a hand through his hair, trying to think, to make sense of this. His whole life had been a lie. He didn't even know who he was anymore. "I don't know if I even want to—well, hell, I don't reckon I even know who I am." He couldn't hide the anguish in his voice.

"Jesse..." With her last ounce of strength, she fought for breath. "You're a smart man, Jesse, you'll find them. Promise me you will, Jesse?" Her eyes fluttered closed, and Jesse waited, his mind refusing to accept the reality of what was happening, what she'd told him.

"I...promise, Ma." He had no idea what he was promising, his mind was too clouded by shock and grief, but he would have promised her anything at this moment.

Grace struggled for one last breath, struggled to open her eyes to see her beloved son one last time. "Oh, Jesse." She clung to his hand, tears clouding her vision of him. "Forgive me, son." She clung to him, not wanting to break this one last connection. "I love you. I've always loved you. You must believe that—" Pain cut off her words, causing her to groan. Her eyes closed and a long, slow breath slipped free and she went very still.

"Mama?" Numb with a host of emotions he couldn't even begin to sort out or understand, his frantic gaze went to the machines. The sounds and motions were slow, sluggish.

"Mama?" He wanted to will life into her, but he knew it was hopeless. "Oh, Ma. I love you." The machines slowly bleeped to a stop until nothing filled the room but unending silence.

Sitting by his mother's bed, still holding her hand, Jesse wept.

## *Chapter One*

*Three months later*
*Saddle Falls, Nevada*

*Jesse was going home.*

Steering his rental car out of the small but bustling Saddle Falls airport parking lot, he adjusted the side- and rearview mirrors, kicked up the air-conditioning, then slipped on his mirrored sunglasses before glancing down at the road map with the directions to the Ryan ranch.

*Home.*

Jesse shook his head as he eased into the flow of traffic leading out of the airport. He wasn't even sure what *home* was anymore; hell, he wasn't even sure who *he* was anymore.

From the moment of his mother's death three months

ago, his entire world had turned upside down. Everything he'd believed about himself and his life had been based on a lie; a lie, that now he was still trying to come to terms with.

Within days of burying his mother, he'd gone to see her lawyer to settle her estate. Still reeling from shock coupled with profound grief, he hadn't known what to do or how to proceed with the information his mother had given him. But he'd made a deathbed promise to her and he'd never broken a promise to Grace—or to anyone—in his life. And he wasn't about to start now, regardless of his own conflicted feelings.

So he'd explained the entire situation to the attorney, who'd offered to discreetly look into the matter for him. It had taken the man three days of research before he'd called with news—news Jesse wasn't certain he was ready to hear.

The attorney believed he was really Jesse Ryan, youngest grandson of ranching patriarch Tommy Ryan of Saddle Falls, Nevada. Saddle Falls was a small but prosperous ranching community about two hours from Las Vegas. Twenty years earlier, at the age of five, Jesse Ryan, the youngest of Tommy Ryan's four grandsons had been kidnapped from his own home while in the care of a nanny, never to be heard from again.

From everything the attorney had discovered, there were too many similarities to Grace's story for Jesse to just dismiss the information. Needing additional confirmation, Jesse had decided to take that first frightening step by placing a call to Tommy Ryan.

Jesse sighed, remembering the conversation. He'd been stunned when the phone had been answered by a man with a definite Irish brogue. Quickly recovering, he'd simply explained who he was and that he was looking for his family—his real family—and had reason to believe he might be Jesse Ryan.

Although that first conversation was fraught with fear on Jesse's part and, of course, a hint of suspicion on Tommy Ryan's part, Jesse knew they both needed more information than could be shared by a simple phone call.

Braking for a stoplight, Jesse pulled out the first letter from Tommy that had arrived by overnight mail the morning after their initial phone conversation. He'd read and reread the letter so many times, it was now dog-eared.

With a sigh, Jesse blew out a frustrated breath. It hadn't been difficult to read the pain and sorrow in Tommy's words. Strangely, he'd felt the first flicker of emotion about the Ryans when he read Tommy's letters. There was an odd tug deep in his heart, a connection that left him totally stunned and confused.

How could he feel a connection to a man he didn't even know? A man who supposedly was his grandfather?

Jesse shook his head. It didn't make any sense to him, but then again, not much in the past three months did.

Tommy's letters had begun arriving without fail once a week. Tommy had done his best to fill Jesse in on the family he didn't know and couldn't remember. Tommy had told him about his three brothers—Jake, Jared and Josh—and included snapshots of them.

It wasn't until Jesse saw the photos of his brothers

that he felt an uncanny sense of recognition deep in the recesses of his memory and in his heart. With a few physical differences, including a few years and maybe a few pounds, looking at those pictures was like looking in a mirror, leaving Jesse feeling oddly disquieted.

Until those photos had arrived, he'd found all the information Tommy had sent him to be just words on paper, distinctly disjointed from who he was or what his life had been.

Or the man he was today.

But he had to admit, spooked or not, those pictures had changed something, touching a chord deep within him, so deep he wasn't certain he was ready to acknowledge it quite yet.

And it also set off an uncomfortable, confusing mix of yearning somewhere in his heart, in a place he never even realized existed—until now.

Perhaps it was because it was the first time he consciously had to consider that perhaps he *was* indeed the missing Jesse Ryan.

And he wasn't entirely sure how he felt about it. Or how to come to terms with it.

He'd stared at those pictures for hours on end, desperately trying to remember them, to remember something—*anything*—from his early childhood—to no avail.

Feeling a roll of tension tighten his gut, Jesse thought once again that taking all of this in and absorbing it was just too much. Hell, just remembering the names of his brothers' wives and assorted children without a scorecard was going to take some effort.

He had never felt very comfortable around a lot of people, so the thought of being part of such a large family was more than enough to give him pause, not to mention an easy reason for putting off this visit.

After three emotionally conflicting months, he'd decided he had no choice. For his own peace of mind, he had to find out the truth—about the Ryans and about himself.

After Tommy Ryan admitted he had checked out Jesse's story and was convinced of his identity, Tommy had repeatedly extended an open-ended invitation for him to come home at any time.

*Home.*

How was he ever going to tell Tommy that he already had a home? Jesse wondered with a frown. Texas was his home, where he'd been nurtured, loved and cared for for as long as he could remember by the only mother—the only family— he'd ever wanted, needed or known?

He hadn't a clue.

Late last night before he could change his mind, he'd called Tommy to tell him he was coming to Saddle Falls—this morning. Delighted, Tommy had laughed his deep, booming laugh and offered to send a plane for him, a car, anything he wanted or needed, but he'd steadfastly refused all of Tommy's offers. He didn't want anything from the Ryans.

He had no need for their money. While he certainly wasn't rich, he was comfortable enough for his needs. He still had the ranch in Texas, and anything and everything else that he required. So there was nothing he wanted, needed or would accept from the Ryans.

Except perhaps a glimpse into who Jesse Ryan had been.

*He was Jesse Garland.*

Had been for as long as he could remember, and Jesse Garland was who he planned to stay, he thought firmly. He'd go to Saddle Falls, meet the Ryans and stay totally, emotionally detached.

It wouldn't be difficult. He was both a loner and a rancher, used to being alone and comfortable with it. He dealt only with facts in his job, steadfastly remaining dispassionate about his men and his animals. He had to, otherwise every time he lost one, he'd be torn up inside. Not a very productive way to run a business.

So he planned to employ with the same detachment with the Ryans he used in his everyday life.

And hope like hell it worked.

Glancing in his rearview mirror before changing lanes to exit the ramp leading to Saddle Falls, Jesse checked the map on the seat next to him before making a right turn, trying to banish his thoughts.

He watched the scenery change as he drove until the busy streets turned into wide, winding country roads dotted with spots of greenery, palm trees and large ranches and farm buildings.

Saddle Falls had pretty scenery, with the top of Mount Charleston gleaming in his rearview mirror as well as a small-town feel to it. Not that much different from his own home in Southwind, Texas.

Glancing at the passing landscape, Jesse knew he wasn't too far from the Ryan ranch, at least according to Tommy's directions. Narrowing his gaze, Jesse slowed the car. A hint of recognition, some sense of having seen all this before, startled him.

He drove slower. He knew the Ryan's ranch was nearby, right at the bottom of the upcoming hill—if he wasn't mistaken.

But it was another house, an aged, sprawling two-story that caught his attention. The house was set on prime acreage, with a lot of land and outbuildings—abandoned now—surrounding it like weary guards on sentry duty.

But the once-glorious white clapboard structure was faded with age and sorely in need of some paint and tender loving care. Set far back from the road, with a long, winding driveway and a landscape of overgrown weeds and greenery, Jesse realized this house was familiar.

He *remembered* this house.

Stunned, he found himself hitting the brakes, straining his neck to get a better look. He knew in his heart he'd not only seen this house before but been inside it. He slipped off his sunglasses to get a better look.

Jesse frowned in thought, wondering how he knew that if he went up the now-sagging back porch, the third step would creak and that the door would open into a cramped mudroom that led directly into a long, sprawling kitchen with faded pine plank flooring.

In his mind's eye he could clearly see the room; hear the slight creak of the third step. A shiver of awareness rippled over Jesse, chilling him in spite of the heat of the day.

He sat there in the car simply staring at the house, willing himself to remember. An image flashed through his mind. An image of a young towheaded girl running around the front of the house, laughing an infectious laugh that carried on the wind.

*Hannah-Anna.*

The name whispered through his mind.

*Hannah-Anna.*

Jesse closed his eyes and he saw her as if she were standing in front of him. A tiny little thing, all spindly arms and legs, bruised and scraped, with long, golden-blond hair that glinted like gold as it flared out behind her, blowing in the wind like a rambunctious flag.

His breath caught as his lids slowly opened. He had to blink several times to be certain he wasn't hallucinating. The little girl he'd just seen in his mind's eye was riding a bright pink-paisley bike with training wheels down the driveway right toward him. Some premonition or recognition swept over him, sending a flurry of emotions racing through him. It was as if this young girl had materialized right from his mind.

*Who was she?*

*Hannah-Anna.*

''You're losing it, boy,'' he muttered to himself, unable to drag his gaze away from the little girl. ''Definitely losing it.''

He watched, unable to contain a smile as the child, who couldn't be more than five or six, stood up on spindly legs to gather enough strength and weight to push the pedals of the almost-too-big-for-her bike, swinging her skinny little body from side to side with a fierce determination that belied her tiny size. Full of concentration, she was biting her lower lip in a way that reminded him of someone else. Who, he wasn't certain.

Unable to drag his gaze away, Jesse pulled to the curb and merely watched the girl, feeling a distinct uneasiness.

*He knew her.*

But he hadn't a clue who she was. *Had* known her, he realized dully. In some other time and place.

His heart constricted, then bumped once, twice as he watched the little girl almost lose her balance and fall.

''Lordy, little lady, if you're not careful you're gonna hurt yourself,'' he muttered, watching as her adorable face screwed up in concentration and her oversize owlish glasses slipped down her nose.

He chuckled as she tried to push up her glasses and keep control of the bike while still pedaling. She might be small, but she was one fierce, determined female, he thought in admiration.

Like someone else he used to know.

*Hannah-Anna.*

The name whispered through his mind again and Jesse shook his head.

He had no idea who Hannah-Anna was.

But he damn sure was going to find out.

''Riley, honey, you stay on the driveway so Mama can see you, you hear?'' Shielding her eyes from the intense afternoon sun, Hannah Grace Myers glanced over toward the wide expanse of driveway to make certain her daughter was still in view. ''I'll be done hanging out these clothes in a minute then we'll have some ice cream before we go to work. Okay, honey?''

Blowing a wisp of blond hair off her own forehead, Hannah swiped the back of her hand against her damp brow, then pulled a clothespin off the clothesline in order to hang the sheet she'd just pulled out of the wicker basket of freshly laundered linens.

"'kay, Mama," came the sweet answer, making Hannah smile. At five, her towheaded angel was no bigger than a fairy with huge blue eyes, an upturned nose, delicate bones and small, fragile features.

"Then we're gonna go to Uncle Tommy's house to play, right?" Riley asked hopefully.

"Yes, honey." Hannah paused to give her daughter all her attention. "Remember Mama explained to you that now, instead of working at the big bookstore in town, Mama's going to work for Uncle Tommy. Do you remember?"

"Cooking, right?" Riley asked with a grin that revealed two missing front teeth.

Hannah laughed. "That's right, honey, cooking. Mama's going to be Uncle Tommy's new cook," she said with a hint of pride. It was a blessing that her godfather, Tommy Ryan, was sorely in need of a cook, and had hired her to do something she loved so much. She was finally going to be able to support herself and Riley and support them well.

"I 'member, mama," Riley replied, struggling to turn her bike back around so she could tackle the long driveway again. Her daughter stopped midturn to glance back at her, her blue eyes shining in excitement. "And I get to go to work with you now, and play with Uncle Tommy, right, Mama?"

"That's right, honey. No more baby-sitters for you,"

Hannah teased with a laugh. ''You get to come to work with me and you can play with Uncle Tommy as well.'' Although Tommy was past eighty, he adored playing with Riley and his numerous assorted great-grandchildren as much as they adored playing with him.

''And I could play with Uncle Jake and Uncle Josh and Uncle Jared—sometimes—when they gots time, right, Mama?''

''That's right, honey.'' Hanging another sheet on the line, Hannah glanced at her daughter, wondering if she needed more sunscreen. The Nevada sun in the afternoon could be brutal, even at the beginning of January. At least there was a faint breeze blowing, giving them some relief.

''Mama?'' Riley hesitated, then said, ''And I could play with Timmy and Terry, and maybe even sometimes Ditka and Ruth, right?'' Her words were so hopeful, her blue eyes shining in expectation, Hannah felt an overwhelming rush of love for her daughter, so strong it nearly staggered her. But then it always did.

She ached for all the things she hadn't been able to provide Riley with, but none more so than a large, loving family of her own.

''Yes, honey, you can play with Timmy and Terry, and even the dogs.''

''Can I get a dog soon?'' Puckering her mouth in concentration, Riley's eyes, wide and innocent behind her large glasses, held a hopeful question, making Hannah sigh. ''I'm big now, Mama. Almost six. And you said I could get a dog when I was big.'' Riley's grin widened at her logic as she struggled to hold the bike upright and still. ''So could I get a dog now?''

Hannah pushed back the bout of guilt that she'd come to think of as the single mother's constant companion. ''That's right, honey, I did promise,'' she admitted, trying not to frown as she hung another sheet. ''But with Mama's new job and you just starting kindergarten, it might be better to wait a while.''

''A while?'' Riley repeated the unknown word with a frown. ''Is that a week, Mama?'' Riley asked hopefully, making Hannah laugh again. They'd been having this same discussion since the first time Riley had laid eyes on Timmy and Terry Ryan's dogs, Ruth and Ditka. Timmy and Terry were Jared Ryan's six-year-old twin sons—and substitute brothers to Riley. And their misbehaved mutts had captured her daughter's heart the moment she'd laid eyes on them.

More than anything in the world, her daughter wanted a dog. And as much as she'd tried to give Riley everything she'd ever wanted or needed, as a single parent responsible for the sole support of herself and her precious daughter, she'd learned to be practical.

And right now, adding an animal to their little family might not be the best thing. They wouldn't have much time to spend with a dog, not to mention the extra expense of another member of the household.

Although her new salary from Tommy was more than generous, allowing for some much-needed necessities and a few indulgent luxuries like the brand spanking new pink two-wheeler Riley was riding, Hannah always erred on the side of caution, especially when it came to financial matters.

"A week?" Hannah repeated, glancing down at her daughter, who had the face of an angel and the occasional temper of a tornado. "Hmm, maybe a bit longer than that, honey," Hannah said, adding another sheet to the clothesline and watching it billow gently in the slight breeze.

"You always say that, Mama," Riley accused with a pout and a long, weary sigh as she struggled to finish turning her new bike back around.

"I know, sweetheart, but remember how I explained that a dog needs to have company? Someone who will be here all day to feed and take care of it."

"Like a baby, huh, Mama?" Riley asked dejectedly. "That's why we can't have a new baby like Terry and Timmy have, right? 'Cuz we can't stay home and take care of it."

Hannah tried not to laugh at her daughter's logic. "That's right, honey." Ever since Jake, Josh and Jared, Tommy's grown grandsons, and their wives had begun having babies, Riley, not wanting to be left out of anything, had been begging for a new baby sister or brother as well.

The thought was so ludicrous it always made Hannah laugh. Explaining to her adorable five-year-old, why she, a twenty-five-year-old single mother barely scraping by couldn't even consider having another baby, let alone that she hadn't either the time nor the inclination to date, or, for that matter, get involved with another man, seemed far too complicated. Explaining her rationale for not getting a dog suddenly seemed far less harmless.

"I'll tell you what, honey. Why don't we wait and

see how school goes first? And then we'll see about getting you a dog. Let's give it a couple of weeks and then we'll talk about it again, okay?''

‘‘'kay,'' Riley said with a sigh, apparently appeased as she climbed back on her bike.

‘‘Stay in the driveway, now,'' Hannah cautioned.

‘‘I will, Mama. I could almost get all the way down the driveway by myself,'' she added proudly, shakily pedaling the bike. Hannah bit her lip, resisting the urge to go to her daughter and help her, knowing that as much as she detested the fact, if she wanted Riley to grow up to be strong and independent, she had to let her do things on her own, at her own speed.

Hannah sighed again, realizing that at times she was too cautious, too overprotective of her only child, but then reality sunk in and she realized that there was no more important job in her life than being a good mother. And if that meant being overprotective of her daughter, so be it.

Besides, she'd never been a gambler or a risk taker. Especially when it came to her daughter. It just wasn't in her nature.

She liked to think of herself as a pragmatic, practical woman who dealt in common sense. It had become a habit to think through every step, every move twice and then calmly and rationally go over everything again just to be certain before she made any decisions.

Only once had Hannah allowed her emotions to overrule her practicality and common sense. Only once had she allowed her own desperate yearning to have a family of her own—a *real* family—get the best of her, and the end result had left her a young, naive, woefully unprepared single mother.

But she'd learned, she thought, glancing affectionately at her daughter again. She'd learned quickly that decisions and actions based on emotion could only lead to innumerable mistakes and heartache.

The end result of her own naiveté had been the loss of her pride, her self-esteem, as well as her family, who'd disowned her for disgracing them by getting pregnant and refusing to marry Riley's father. Before she and her parents could reconcile, they'd been killed in a boating accident, but they had left Riley their house—in trust. Hannah never knew if that was their way of saying they'd forgiven her or not. She didn't dwell on it because the pain of their words, their anger and disappointment had never faded. She'd never apologize for bringing Riley into the world. Not to anyone.

Well, the reason Hannah wouldn't marry the man was that not only had he never asked, he had also never once mentioned that he was already married and had a family. Riley's father hadn't been interested in the family he already had, let alone a new one. Although Hannah felt guilty sometimes for depriving her precious daughter of a father, she figured in the long run she hadn't robbed Riley of too much except a whole lot of disappointment and heartache from a man who hadn't wanted Riley and couldn't or wouldn't accept her.

Despite the loss and the painful life lessons, Hannah had received an incredible gain—a beautiful, loving daughter who filled every need in her heart.

Biting her lower lip, Hannah wondered if the career decision she'd made so recently had been made with her usual practical common sense. Or a bit of emotion. Perhaps it had been both, she considered, hanging the last sheet out to dry.

She'd been an accomplished cook since the age of twelve and loved creating beautiful meals, so having a job doing something she loved seemed perfect. The salary Tommy had offered was more than generous, and with his longtime housekeeper/cook, Mrs. Taylor, finally retiring, accepting the job would also allow her to spend more time with Riley since she could bring her to work with her.

It was, Hannah realized, a dream come true. Enough money to support them, a job she loved and more time to spend with her daughter.

So why was she worried? she wondered, trying to shake off her own concerns.

Perhaps it was that she always worried that she was taking advantage of Tommy and his family. As her godfather, it was Tommy who'd always been there for her, including her in his own family, making her feel welcome, wanted and loved, something her own parents never had time for, even *before* they disowned her.

Although she'd been a bit younger than Jake, Jared and Josh, they'd always treated her like the sister they'd never had, and Riley like one of their own children, giving both a sense of belonging.

Having the Ryans in their lives gave Riley a sense of being part of a huge, loving family, the one thing—the *only* thing—Hannah wasn't able to provide for her daughter on her own.

With another sigh, Hannah hung the last pillowcase on the clothesline. Unconsciously, her gaze traveled to the driveway and she felt an instant of panic. Riley's bike was lying on its side, pink streamers blowing in the afternoon breeze.

But her daughter was nowhere to be seen.

"Riley?" Hannah stepped over the now-empty laundry basket, knocking it over and wiping her suddenly damp hands on her jean shorts. "Riley!" she called louder, trying not to panic. Her daughter knew better than to leave the driveway.

"Mama! Mama, come see. This man looks like Uncle Jake." Riley's voice drifted back toward her and Hannah patted her heart to calm it as she stalked down the driveway, coming to a halt when she saw a stranger holding her daughter's hand.

With his large buff-colored Stetson, his faded jeans, boots, and chambray shirt, he could have passed for Jake Ryan's twin.

*But it wasn't Jake Ryan,* Hannah realized instantly.

He was a bit taller than Jake, built a bit bigger, and he was clearly younger than Jake, but he had the same inky-black hair curling over the collar of his shirt. And the same incredible Ryan blue eyes.

And a face that couldn't deny he *was* a Ryan.

While all the Ryan men were undeniably gorgeous, Hannah had always felt more sisterly toward them. She could acknowledge and appreciate their good looks, but had never felt that instinctive female stirring of lust that looking at *this man* had curling in her gut. The strength of the sensation reminded her that in spite of her deliberately man-devoid life, she was still a young woman and still had all the needs and desires she'd been trying to ignore since Riley's birth.

And she wasn't particularly pleased that those needs and desires had picked *this* particular moment to rear their rambunctious heads.

She took a long, slow breath and let her breath out slowly before stepping closer. There were prickles of fear, awareness and a host of other confusing feelings swamping her, and she wasn't quite certain how to react to them.

Or to the incredibly gorgeous hunk of male holding her precious daughter's hand.

*''Hannah-Anna.''*

Unaware he'd even spoken, Jesse stared at the adult version of the adorable little girl. Everything seemed to slow, then still inside him—except his heart. It gave a solid bump, then sped up as if it were on a racecourse. The entire world faded away and there was only her, standing there like an apparition.

*Hannah-Anna.*

A kaleidoscope of emotions, feelings, memories converged all at once, nearly staggering him, flashing instantly through his mind like a movie that had been fast-forwarded at warp speed.

He saw her as she'd been; the adorable, mischievous girl he'd played tag with, chased around and around her house. He remembered, and could almost hear, her squeals of delight echoing behind her as she ran as fast as her legs could carry her, no match for his longer, stronger ones as he caught her, held her, tickled her or pulled her hair.

Or protected her when anyone else dare tease her.

*It was Hannah-Anna.*

*His Hannah-Anna.*

•

Jesse was almost certain he'd stopped breathing. Surely the earth had stopped moving and time must have stood still as he simply stood there staring at her. The memory of her had snuck up on him, catching him totally off guard.

Giving his head a shake, he let his eyes close for a moment to gather himself, then slowly opened them, surprised that she was still standing there staring at him as if she'd seen a ghost.

She was all grown up and the most beautiful thing he'd ever seen. His heart kept hammering wickedly as his gaze slowly traipsed over her, wanting—needing to see every inch of her.

Small and delicate, she had a mass of wavy, golden-blond hair that flowed down her back. Her eyes, a vibrant, vivid blue rimmed by thick black lashes reminded him of a clear Texas sky on a summer day. Wide open and at the moment clouded by some emotion he couldn't read.

She wore a pair of shorts that hugged an incredibly sexy butt and revealed a slim expanse of tanned legs long enough to make a man drool. Her feet were sexily bare, and the shirt she had on was the color of ripe apricots and tied just under her breasts, revealing a flat expanse of equally tanned tummy.

Because his throat had gone as dry as the desert, Jesse had to swallow several times before speaking.

''*Hannah-Anna,*'' he whispered again. The deep timbre of his voice was husky with emotion and an unmistakable Texas drawl.

Hannah hadn't heard her childhood nickname in twenty years, not since Jesse Ryan had disappeared.

"J-Jesse?" she whispered, her voice so dry it came out like a croak. Her gaze went over him as he slowly removed his Stetson, allowing a tumble of rich, black hair to fall free, only emphasizing the beautiful shape and sculpture of his chiseled features.

*Ryan features.*

"Jesse," she said again as her lids slid closed and her hand lifted to smother the sob that struggled for freedom. "Oh my God, Jesse." It had been so long since she'd allowed herself to say or even think his name because she'd been unable to bear the tremendous pain and grief the mere thought of his disappearance brought on.

Grief that, as a child, she hadn't known how to handle or what to do with. How does a five-year-old cope with the knowledge that her best friend—her only friend—has disappeared and that she'll never see him again?

It had been too heavy a loss for someone so young to understand or to carry. So she'd buried the pain deep inside her heart, where it had been covered over by other losses, more grief from a life and a family that had not turned out as she'd wanted, expected or needed.

"My God, Jesse, I can't believe it." Her voice was stronger now, but she couldn't stop staring at him, tears streaming down her face as her pulse raced like a runaway train.

"Please don't cry," he said gently, taking a step closer and tenderly wiping a tear from her cheek. Stunned by her reaction to his slight touch, Hannah let her lids lower as she savored the feelings storming through her. When he'd touched her, she'd felt a tingle of electricity strong enough to light up six counties.

With any other man such a reaction would have sent her running in the opposite direction as fast as her legs could carry her. But this was Jesse, she reminded herself. And Jesse had always been different, special to her.

"Jesse, is it really you?" she asked. Stepping closer, Hannah knew she had to touch him, just to assure herself he was here and he was real.

Through eyes blurred with tears she tipped her head back to look at him, then laid her hands on the broad expanse of his chest, feeling her pulse—and his heart—jump in response.

Jesse sighed, a little off balance, a little frightened by the feelings, as well as the memories, swarming over him. Memories he never realized had been buried somewhere within and now could not be ignored or denied, a fact that only added to his emotional confusion.

As did the sight and touch of this incredibly beautiful woman.

"Yeah, darlin', I reckon it's really me." He smiled at her and Hannah was certain someone had hitched the sun a notch. The world somehow seemed brighter. More beautiful.

Hannah didn't think, she couldn't, she merely reacted, throwing her arms around his waist and burying her face in his chest, holding on to him as if she could hold him to her forever.

"Oh, Jesse, I thought I'd never see you again."

"I know, darlin', sorta seemed that way, didn't it?"

he said, not knowing exactly how to respond to her. With her lush, curvy little body pressed against his, he found his own body reacting and responding in a way that shocked him. Since his mother's death three months ago, he hadn't felt anything, it was as if he'd gone cold and dead inside.

Until now.

Until he'd touched her.

Unable to resist, he stroked his free hand down the long curtain of her hair simply to see if it was as soft as it looked. It was.

She was close enough for her deliciously feminine scent to tease him. It was an erotically feminine mixture of heat, sun and woman. He inhaled deeply, wanting to brand the scent into his mind, his memory.

"Welcome home, Jesse." Hannah lifted her tear-stained face and gave him a big, watery smile. "Welcome home."

## *Chapter Two*

*Home.*

It was as if she'd thrown a bucket of cold water on him. Instinctively, Jesse drew back from her, still watching her, not certain this was the time or the place to explain…what? Well hell, he thought in frustration, to explain that he wasn't *home,* home was in Texas. He was merely here for a visit.

And a short visit at that.

Nothing more.

Once he'd satisfied himself that he'd done the right thing, honored his promise to his mother to find his real family, he'd go back home to Texas.

But he wasn't certain this was the time or place to get into it, not with this beautiful woman and adorable little girl looking at him with a mixture of joy and adoration.

"He rescued me, Mama," Riley said with a grin, glancing up at Jesse in adoration. "I almost felled down off my bike but he caught me." Riley's free hand went to her mother's face and her blue eyes rounded in alarm. "Why are you crying, Mama?" she asked. "Are you sad, Mama?"

"Don't worry, darlin'," he said gently. Something about this little tyke had touched his heart the moment he'd lifted her into his arms after she'd nearly crash-landed onto the pavement. She'd trustingly wound her arms around him and was now holding on to his hand as tight as her mother had just a few moments before. "I don't think your mama's sad. I think she's happy, honey."

Aware she was frightening her daughter, Hannah wiped away her tears and smiled. "Jesse's right, honey, I'm not sad." She swiped her damp face again, slipping her shaking hands into the pockets of her shorts. "I'm happy, very happy," she added, unable to drag her gaze away from Jesse's.

"Riley, honey, do you remember Mama told you that a long, long time ago when I was a little girl, right about your age, I had a best friend whose name was Jesse? He was Uncle Jake, Uncle Jared and Uncle Josh's youngest brother?" Hannah reached out and straightened one of her daughter's pigtails. It had come loose from her morning of play.

Riley's eyebrows scrunched together as she tried to concentrate on remembering. "He went away, right?" she asked, then grinned at her mother's nod. "And you never got to play with him again?"

"That's right," Hannah said, blowing a wad of hair

off her face. ''Well, Riley, this is Jesse. Your *Uncle* Jesse.''

''Did you come back to play with my mama again, Uncle Jesse?'' Riley asked with wide-eyed innocence, making Hannah flush and Jesse laugh.

''Well, darlin', I guess you could say that.'' His gaze shifted to Hannah's and she saw the mischievous male twinkle in his eyes, a twinkle that had been there even as a boy, a twinkle that revealed his incredible sense of humor.

She was unbearably pleased to see that it still remained, but felt a bit skittish at the hint of masculine interest she saw there. And the fact that she was readily responding to it.

She'd do well to remember the vow she'd made when she found herself alone and pregnant. She would never allow herself to be vulnerable to a man's charms again. Never again would she fall blindlessly, heedlessly in love, especially with a man who didn't want or value his family. No, she'd come from a family like that, and wanted no part of it or any man who didn't share her love and appreciation for what family meant. If and when she ever took another chance on love, it would have to be with a man who wanted and would treasure the kind of family and family life Tommy Ryan had created.

Finding a man like that was going to take a miracle, and Hannah was fresh out of believing in miracles, so she'd resolved to raise her daughter alone and be alone rather than risk her heart or her daughter's ever again.

Still, looking at Jesse, remembering the closeness they'd once shared, Hannah felt her own female yearnings spring to life, yearnings she'd buried a long time ago. They both annoyed and embarrassed her.

"Well, Miss Riley," Jesse began, his intense masculine gaze still on Hannah's, making her feel a rush of warmth as well as a stirring of female desire she could only categorize as pure, blind lust. It had been so long, she was surprised she recognized it, she thought in amusement. "I guess you could say…uh…playing with your mama just might be one of the things I came back for." Tucking his tongue in his cheek, he rocked back on the heels of his boots as Hannah's face flamed.

With a laugh, she shook her head. Jesse was as charming as the rest of his brothers, but unlike Jake, Jared and Josh, she found herself responding to Jesse, something she knew she couldn't do. She'd simply pretend to ignore whatever electricity was arcing between them. If she ignored it, she wouldn't have to deal with it or worry about it.

"Well, Jesse, it's nice to know some things haven't changed," she said with a smile. "You still have a wicked sense of humor."

"Hannah," he said carefully, not wanting there to be any confusion. "Make no mistake. Everything has changed." His face slowly sobered as he took in his surroundings with an uneasy glance. "I've changed." He brought his eyes back to hers. "I'm not Jesse Ryan," he said quietly but firmly, sending a chill over her, dashing all the warm feelings. "At least not the Jesse Ryan you remember." Frustrated, he dragged a hand through his hair and blew out a breath. "Hell, at the moment, I don't know who I am."

"Mama, Uncle Jesse said a bad word."

"Uh, yes, honey, I know," Hannah said, banking a smile.

Riley turned to Jesse. "You're not supposed to say bad words, Uncle Jesse. They're not pul-lite."

"You're absolutely right, Miss Riley," Jesse said, struggling to smother a smile as well. He gave Hannah a quick, amused glance before bringing his gaze, somber now, back to the indignant imp. "I'm not supposed to use bad words. My mama taught me better than that, and I sure do apologize."

With a frown, Riley continued to study him before turning to her mother, her eyes clouded in confusion. "Mama, are you sure he's not Uncle Jake?" Riley shook her head, setting her pigtails waving to and fro. "'Cuz Uncle Jake says bad words sometimes, too. And he really *looks* like Uncle Jake."

Hannah laughed at her daughter's logic, completely understanding her confusion. "Well, honey, that's because Uncle Jesse is Uncle Jake's brother."

Riley's face brightened. "So if we get a new baby sister or brother for me, will it look like me?"

"That's right, sweetheart," Hannah said with a laugh, realizing Jesse was still studying her. Knowing those glorious, gorgeous blue eyes were appraising, measuring her, made her incredibly nervous. She shrugged to hide it. "Well, Jesse, I'm sorry, but you *do* look just like Jake."

He nodded, struggling to digest that information. "That's what I've gathered."

She studied him for a moment, a flicker of something close to apprehension settling in. "You don't remember?'' she asked quietly. ''You don't remember your brothers?'' she asked, trying to hide her horror at the mere thought.

Jesse blew out a frustrated breath and shook his head slowly. ''No, ma'am, I reckon I don't.''

A thousand questions suddenly sprang to Hannah's mind. None of which had any answers. Where had he been?

Where had he lived?

Who'd raised him?

What had his life been like?

*Why hadn't he come home?*

Struggling to hide her concern, Hannah searched for a safer topic, something that would give her a moment to regain her footing. Realizing she'd introduced Jesse to Riley, but not vice versa, she forced a smile past her nerves as she continued the introductions. ''Jesse, this is my daughter, Riley.''

''Well, Miss Riley,'' Jesse said. ''I'm always happy to meet such a pretty little lady.''

''I'm five,'' Riley offered, holding up one sticky hand and spreading her fingers. ''And I get to go to kindergarten in a few weeks.''

''You do? Kindergarten?'' Jesse drew back, pretending to be surprised. ''Well, then, I reckon you're a pretty lucky little lady, and almost all grown up too, aren't you, darlin'?'' He kissed one of her outstretched fingers.

''Timmy and Terry said kindergarten isn't so bad.'' Fear clouded the child's blue eyes and Jesse felt a tug at his heart. ''I get to ride on a big yellow bus with all the big kids.'' She glanced up at him, her eyes wide.

"But Mama doesn't get to go." Fiercely she shook her head. "I get to go all by myself 'cuz I'm big now, right, Mama?"

Hannah's heart began to ache at the fear shadowed in her daughter's eyes. Oh how she wished she could just wrap her daughter in her arms and protect her from anything and everything that would ever hurt her or be unpleasant.

"That's right, sweetheart," Hannah said with a smile.

He pressed another reassuring kiss to one of Riley's sticky little fingers. "Well now, Miss Riley, I reckon you're going to have a fine time on that big yellow school bus. Just think of all the new friends you'll meet. And then when you come home you can tell your mama here all about your adventures each day."

"Can I tell you, too, Uncle Jesse?" Riley asked hopefully.

"Absolutely, darlin'," Jesse assured her, not wanting to disappoint the child by telling her he probably wouldn't even be here by the time she started school.

"You talk funny," Riley blurted in response.

"Riley!" Hannah almost groaned, but Jesse merely laughed at her daughter's antics, plopping his Stetson on her golden head. It drooped down, covering her eyes, until she pushed it back so she could see.

"Well, darlin', I guess I do talk funny, but then again, where I come from I imagine they'd think you all talk a bit funny as well," he said, punctuating his words by tickling her belly and making her giggle.

"Where do you come from?" Riley asked, wide-eyed, and Hannah wanted to groan again, but Jesse smiled indulgently.

"Texas, honey. I'm from Texas."

"I don't know where that's at," Riley said, pushing his Stetson back farther on her head.

"Is that where you've been, Jesse?" Hannah asked quietly. "In Texas?"

"For as long as I can remember," he admitted with a shrug and a slow, sexy smile that made her toes curl in the small patch of grass she was standing in.

"Do you remember anything, Jesse?" she pressed carefully. "Anything about your life here in Saddle Falls?" Her words caused her heart to beat in trepidation. "Before you went to Texas?"

"You," he said quietly, letting his gaze meet hers, making her heart tumble over again. "I remember you. And I don't exactly reckon why." Confused, he shook his head. "I hadn't remembered anything until I was driving down the road, and then..." He glanced around, trying to absorb his surroundings. "I remembered this house—something about it..."

She chuckled softly to hide her nerves. "That's probably because you spent so much time here. Almost as much time as I spent over at the Ryans'."

He was still studying his surroundings, wondering if doing that would jog more memories. "I didn't know what I remembered about this house. Except that as I drove by, I knew it, knew too that the third step on the back porch used to creak—"

"Still does," Hannah admitted with a laugh, surprised that he would remember something so insignificant.

''And I remembered a little girl named Hannah-Anna,'' he said quietly, tilting his head to continue to study her.

She forced a smile past the sadness that had surfaced. ''It's been twenty years since anyone has called me that, and you, Jesse, were the only one who ever did.'' Clearly, he didn't remember her, not in the same way she remembered him. And it hurt, she realized. Very much.

''I'm sorry,'' he said, not certain he knew what he was sorry about. He only knew her eyes had shadowed at his words and he felt responsible somehow.

''Oh, Jesse, don't be sorry. It's all right.'' She pressed her hands to his chest again, wanting to touch him, to comfort and ease the pain and confusion she saw in his eyes. It only increased the ache in her heart. For him. For her. And especially for the Ryans.

If it hurt this much for Jesse not to remember her, she couldn't even imagine the pain Tommy would endure, knowing his own grandson didn't remember him.

And Jesse *didn't* remember her, not really. And he probably didn't remember the special bond that had always been between them, a bond that at one time she'd been certain would never be broken.

Now she wasn't certain of anything.

''Do you remember the last time you saw me?'' she asked, cocking her head to look at him curiously.

He was thoughtful for a moment, and then images flashed before him and he saw her standing on the sidewalk looking lost and forlorn, crying. The memories flashed quickly, brightly, barely giving him time to absorb them.

"We were playing hide-and-seek out behind the main house here." Lost in the images of his memory, he spoke by rote, not certain where the words or the memories were coming from. "It was summer and hotter than blazes. We were both running around barefoot. We'd run under the sprinkler just to cool off before we went on with our game." He had to stop, to swallow because his mouth was so dry. "But I had to be home before dark. I was walking backward down the sidewalk toward my house, waving, and feeling bad because you were standing out front, crying because I had to go home."

The word slammed into him.

*Home.*

*He'd had to go home.*

Absently, he rubbed his forehead where a dull ache had started. Apparently there were some long-buried memories deep inside the recesses of his mind.

"That's right, Jesse," Hannah said, encouraged. "That night I was standing on the front porch waving and crying because you had to go home." She had to swallow around the sudden lump in her throat at the painful memory. "That was the last time I saw you. You disappeared that night." She brushed a fresh tear from her cheek, the loss as fresh today as it had been twenty years ago. "Jesse," she began carefully. "Do you remember anything else? Anything about your family?"

How could he tell her he knew who Jesse Garland was, who Jesse Garland's family was, knew who he was supposed to be, knew what was expected of him, and knew too how he'd act or react in any given situation.

However, he didn't remember anything about Jesse Ryan.

And he didn't know if he truly wanted to know because then if he knew, he might have to deal with it and accept it, and accept all that went along with becoming Jesse Ryan—Tommy Ryan's youngest grandson.

And that meant turning his back on who he'd been his whole life, as well as the woman who'd loved him, raised him as her own. Love and loyalty weren't just words to him, but something a man—an honorable man—never turned his back on.

He was still reeling from his mother's death, her confession, and then all these months trying to absorb the information he'd learned once he'd found out about Tommy Ryan and his missing grandson.

It was far too much for him to take in and accept right now. It was coming too fast, without enough time for him to absorb it or put into perspective.

Maybe coming here had been a mistake, he thought, staring at Hannah. Maybe he hadn't really been ready for what he might learn or have to face.

And he was certain he hadn't been prepared for her, nor for the gut-level male reaction he was having to her.

Just another emotion to add to the confusing mix.

He shook his head. "No," he said firmly, not certain of much at the moment, but certain of this if nothing else. "I don't remember anything about them."

"Them?" One eyebrow rose and Hannah watched

him carefully, not certain what it was in his eyes. Wariness, of course, a hint of fear, and something else she couldn't read. It sent a chill through her. "You don't remember your grandfather, Tommy, or your brothers, Jake, Jared or Josh?"

He shook his head, then blew out a breath. "Hannah, the only family I ever had was my mother, Grace, and she passed away going on three months back now."

Hannah couldn't help it, her temper flared, fueled by fear and frustration. "Jesse, I don't know who this Grace person was, but your family is the Ryans. *You're a Ryan,*" she insisted, temper in her words. Unconsciously, her hands fisted in his shirt as she struggled to contain the floodgate of emotions his words had opened.

Tommy Ryan had spent twenty years praying—waiting—for the day when Jesse would be found, would come home. How would he handle knowing Jesse didn't even remember him?

Or worse, far worse, wouldn't *accept* him?

She loved and adored her godfather. He was the finest man she'd ever met, the kind of man she'd always wished had been her father. She wouldn't want anything or anyone—not even his youngest, beloved grandson—to hurt him.

A strong streak of protectiveness rose in Hannah and she wanted to shake Jesse, shake him until he realized what his lack of acceptance of Tommy might do to the man. And to the entire Ryan family, who had spent twenty years grieving for him, searching for him, loving him.

She knew firsthand how the rejection of your family—for any reason—hurt, cutting a path through your heart that never truly healed. She knew because she'd lived with it for as long as she could remember, even before her daughter's birth.

She wanted to protect Tommy and all the Ryans from ever feeling such heartache and despair.

"No," Jesse countered quietly but just as firmly. "I'm a *Garland.* Jesse *Garland,*" he emphasized. "My family was Grace Garland, and she's gone."

Hannah forced herself to take a slow, deep breath because emotion had her words and voice shaking. "Your mother's name was Janice and your father's name was Jock. Your parents were killed in a plane crash almost fifteen years ago."

He merely stared at her, realizing her words meant nothing. He shrugged. "I'm sorry, but I don't remember anyone named Janice or Jock." He shrugged again at the look on her face. "Sorry."

"Jesse," she said, trying again. "Your father, Jock, was your grandfather Tommy's only son, his only child." The strength of her words surprised her. She hadn't realized how desperately she wanted him to remember his life and family here. Or how desperately she wanted things to be the way they once were. Not for her sake, but for Tommy's. "You don't remember Tommy, your parents or your brothers or anything else?" she asked, thoroughly frustrated.

He shook his head, still studying his surroundings because looking at her made him feel things he wasn't certain he understood. Male feelings, feelings that had nothing to do with who he was or who she was. Feelings that were purely male responding to female.

And there were far too many emotions swirling around inside his mind, his heart, to add any more to the mix. Emotional overload his mother would have called it.

He glanced at Hannah again. She was the most incredibly beautiful woman he'd ever seen in his life. But she was someone from his past, someone from Jesse Ryan's life.

Not his.

*He was Jesse Garland.*

Jesse Ryan wasn't someone he knew or understood, nor was he certain he wanted to know or understand who he'd been. Nor did he like the emotions that this woman aroused in him. They were far too strong and just as frightening. But he couldn't deny there was some kind of emotional connection, something that seemed to be drawing him closer to her, wanting to be closer to her.

And it scared the hell out of him.

He knew he couldn't allow his emotions free rein. He was here for one reason and one reason only: to honor his late mother's wishes.

Jesse Garland was who he knew. He understood Jesse Garland, knew his history, his past, knew everything about him. Jesse Garland was who he was comfortable with, and that wasn't about to change now, not because of a few remembered memories.

Or a childhood friend.

He'd do well to remember that.

Besides, he wasn't here for the long haul. A short visit and he was on his way back home. The thought helped to soothe some of his emotional turmoil.

''I'm thirsty, Mama.'' Riley rolled her eyes. ''Real thirsty. And you said we could have some ice cream before we went to Uncle Tommy's.'' Riley bent and scratched a mosquito bite on her knee.

At Jesse's surprised look, Hannah felt the need to explain. ''I work for Tommy. As his cook,'' she clarified, lifting her hands out of her shorts pockets to wipe them on the jean material. She hadn't realized how nervous she was until now. ''Mrs. Taylor, Tommy's cook, finally retired, and he offered me the job. So I took it,'' she added with a shrug. If she expected some hint of recognition at the mention of Mrs. Taylor, she was disappointed. Jesse gave no reaction.

''Well, I guess I'd better get going then,'' Jesse said with a slow, lazy smile that sent her pulse scrambling. As much as he'd dreaded the actual meeting with Tommy Ryan, meeting Hannah had stirred him up just as much and he felt the need to leave, to take some time to put things in perspective. ''I've taken up enough of your time.''

''Wait, Jesse.'' Hannah touched his arm before turning to her daughter, indicating she wanted to speak to him. Alone. ''Sweetheart, why don't you go inside and get yourself some of the cookies Mama baked this morning?''

''Can I have three?'' Riley asked, holding up three fingers and making Jesse smile.

''Yes, honey, but only three. Remember, we're going to take them over to Uncle Tommy's with us, and besides, I don't want you to ruin your dinner.'' She gave her daughter's backside an affectionate pat. ''Go on now, I'll put your bike away for you.''

"Thanks, Mama." Riley lifted her face to Jesse's and gifted him with a brilliant smile. "Bye, Uncle Jesse." She waved several fingers at him. He waved back.

"Bye, Miss Riley," he said with a smile. "It sure was a pleasure meeting you."

She giggled again, then skipped off toward the back porch. Hannah waited until the door shut behind Riley before turning to Jesse.

"She's a beautiful little girl," Jesse said, surprising her. "Her daddy must be real proud of her."

Hannah stiffened. "Riley doesn't have a daddy. She has me, and I'm all she needs."

Well now, Jesse thought, glancing at Hannah curiously. There was more than a little resentment laced through those words, he thought. It was curious. What kind of man walked away from a beautiful child like that? he wondered. Certainly no man he'd ever known. Or wanted to know.

"Jesse, please, listen to me." Unconsciously, Hannah wrung her hands together to gather her thoughts. The last thing she wanted was to get into a discussion of her personal life—or, rather, lack of it. Or her marital status or lack of it. Or Riley's parental situation—or lack of it, realizing that in spite of the years that had passed she still felt a bit of shame at having been so young, so stupid and so very duped. Her personal life was not the point. Right now she wanted—needed—to talk to him about Tommy.

"Jesse, look, I can understand how difficult this must be for you—" His chuckle caught her by surprise and she glanced up at him. "What? What's so funny?"

Annoyance tinged her tone and he slowly shook his head again.

"Trust me, darlin', there is no way anyone could have a clue how difficult all this is. You grow up believing you're one person, and then one day you're supposed to accept that you're another person, with a whole different family history..." His voice trailed off. "And you think you know how difficult this is? There's no way anyone could understand what I'm feeling because, to tell you the truth, darlin', I sure as hell don't understand it myself."

The impact of his words had Hannah rethinking what she was going to say. "Jesse, I'm sorry," she said quietly. "It's just, Tommy has spent twenty years looking for you, grieving for you, and I don't want to see him hurt."

Jesse nodded. "I understand that, Hannah, and I'm not here to hurt the man. Truly." He shrugged. "But you've got to understand, it wasn't me he was grieving for, it was the boy who was his grandson, a little boy named Jesse who disappeared twenty years ago. And from the moment he disappeared, that boy was gone. He became someone else. Grew up to be someone else. That someone else is me, Hannah, Jesse Garland. Try as I might, I can't change the past nor can I change who and what I am."

"Jesse, please, just promise me you won't hurt him." The pleading in her eyes tugged at something deep inside Jesse and made him reach out and gently lay his hand against her cheek.

"Darlin', I wish I could promise that, I truly do," he said quietly, his gaze firmly on hers. "But I'm not a man who makes a promise he isn't certain he can keep."

Her eyes flashed like the fires of hell and her fists balled at her hips. "Jesse, I'm warning you, watch your step. I'll not stand by and watch you deliberately hurt Tommy." She took another step closer, her eyes gleaming with intensity. "I mean it."

He merely stared at her, surprised by the depth of her fierceness, the loyalty and love he saw shimmering off her in waves. He admired a woman who knew the value of loyalty and honesty, as well as a woman who could love that deeply, freely, intensely.

Unconsciously, he glanced at her hands, saw they were ringless and wondered about Riley's father. Again. This was a woman who wouldn't take love, loyalty or honesty lightly. For some reason he found it warmed something within his scarred heart.

After his mother's deception, he'd feared that all women were dishonest about love, loyalty and family. Hell, if he hadn't been able to trust his own mother, how could he ever trust any other woman?

Maybe this woman was a woman worth trusting.

It was a shame he wasn't going to be around long enough to find out.

"Well then, Hannah," he said softly, never taking his gaze off hers as he settled his Stetson more comfortably on his head. "I guess I'll consider myself properly warned."

## *Chapter Three*

Tommy Ryan was nervous.

He hadn't paced this much since the impending birth of his last great-grandchild, but then again, he thought as he paused on the front porch and cocked his head to see if he'd heard a car, it wasn't every day a man was reunited with a grandson missing for twenty years.

With a sigh of impatience, Tommy shook his head as he continued to pace the long front porch of the main ranch house he'd built nearly fifty years ago. He'd waited twenty years for this day; he supposed he could wait a bit longer. But it was hard, he realized with a self-indulgent chuckle. Very hard. He felt like one of the little lads waiting for Christmas morning to come.

Lifting his head, he glanced around at all that was his and he couldn't help but smile, a smile of pride and accomplishment.

He'd arrived in this country from Ireland with little more than the clothes on his back and a fierce determination to build something of his own. An empire, of course, but more importantly, a family.

A man's wealth and his true worth would always be his family, he thought, glancing at the empty road again and resisting the urge to sigh impatiently.

He'd accomplished everything he'd ever dreamed of, needed. He had more wealth than any man had a want for, and more possessions than any one man could crave, but through it all, he'd lost one of the most important parts of his life: his youngest grandson, Jesse.

Cursing his bad hip, Tommy leaned on his wood-carved cane as he lowered himself into one of the rockers his grandson Jared had carved with his own hands for his wife to rock their babes.

In spite of a bad hip, at eighty, Tommy still had the large, powerful build of the boxer he had once been, a build that had intimidated more than its fair share of stout men over the years.

Age and infirmity had not stooped his frame, but merely slowly his gait. His hair, which had been a thick mane of coal in his youth, was now a thick shock of white framing his face like an elegant halo. His skin was a rich, deep tan, lined with the experience and memories of his long life.

His mouth was full and firm and more often than not curved into a grin, as if he had a secret he wasn't quite ready to share with the world yet. His blue eyes, the color of the deepest sapphires, still twinkled with mischief most of the time, giving him the appearance of a slightly oversize leprechaun.

There was an air of power and authority radiating from him, the kind that only very successful men possess.

He was a man who'd been blessed with more luck than any man deserved, more money then he could ever hope to spend and a family he adored more than life itself.

But interspersed in the joys of his life had been sorrow. A deep, aching sorrow that no amount of joy could erase.

But today, finally, the ache in his heart would heal, and he and his beloved grandson would be reunited. He'd sent everyone else off for the day, wanting some time alone with the lad, and hoping to ease the way for Jesse so he wouldn't be overwhelmed.

''You're finally coming home, lad,'' Tommy whispered to himself, vowing not to let free the tears he'd held so long in his heart. ''I've waited so long for this day, my boy, so long. It's a dream come true.'' Sniffling, Tommy pulled a large pressed handkerchief from his pocket—just in case—and dabbed briskly at his nose. ''You'll not be dripping tears like a spoiled babe in front of the lad, Tommy boy,'' he scolded himself. '''Tis a day for laughter not tears. Aye, it's a day for the angels to sing and to rejoice.'' Tommy paused a moment to wipe his eyes, which were damp with memories and emotion.

Oh how he wished his only son, Jock, was still alive to see this day. To know that his youngest had finally come home. Jock had died without ever knowing the fate of his youngest son. It was a heartache Jock had never gotten over, and a heartache Tommy had been forced to live with; a pain that had never eased.

Tommy glanced heavenward. The sky was a clear crystal-blue, and he was fairly certain if he stared long and hard enough, he might be able to see the angels rejoicing. He couldn't help but smile.

"Aye, Jock, my boy, you can finally rest easy now," he whispered to the heavens. "I told you I'd not rest nor meet my maker until I found the lad." Tommy thumped his cane and nodded his head. "Aye, your Da never made a promise he couldn't keep. A wise man doesn't. It took me a good long time, but I've kept my promise to you, Jock, and to myself." Tommy had to pause to swipe at his eyes again. "Our boy Jesse, we've found him, Jock. He's coming home."

The sound of a car coming down the hill had Tommy leaning on his cane to stand and stare. His heart began to thud loudly and he found it difficult to take a breath. Shading his eyes with his hand, Tommy's heart did a slow drumbeat as he watched a large black truck approach, and finally pull slowly into the long winding driveway. With the sun in his eyes, he couldn't really see the driver.

Until he got out.

Then everything inside Tommy Ryan seemed to still as he looked at one of his own.

He stood immobilized on the front porch, clutching his cane with one strong hand, then laid his other hand to his heart as he watched the young man step slowly, hesitantly, out of the truck.

There was no mistaking this lad. He had his father's great height, and was clearly the tallest of all four of

Jock's sons. He possessed Tommy's own twinkling blue eyes, eyes the same color as the Irish Sea shortly after a storm. But most importantly, he had his brothers' features. All of his brothers, mixed together in a face that was undeniably a Ryan.

The young man started walking up the driveway, then paused. "Tommy Ryan?" The voice was deep, husky with suppressed emotion and still familiar to Tommy, in spite of the Texas twang and seemed to reverberate in the air between them, closing the distance. The young lad's voice had the same deep resonance of his brothers'. Tommy wanted to kick up his heels in glee.

"My God," Tommy whispered, pressing his hand tighter against his chest, as if to ease the ache in his heart. "Jesse. 'Tis you." It could have been a hundred years since he'd last seen the lad, but he'd recognize him anywhere; it was like recognizing his own soul. His own kin.

Joy bubbled within him like champagne and Tommy fervently wished for a good hip, for he'd have done an Irish jig right there on the front porch, a jig to make the Ryan clan proud.

It *was* Jesse; *his* Jesse.

Standing on Ryan land once again.

As it should be; as it was meant to be.

"Aye, Jock," Tommy whispered with a smile and a slow shake of his head as he glanced heavenward for a brief moment. "He's come home."

With a silent, heartfelt prayer of thanks, Tommy let his breath out slowly, and with it all the fear, loneliness, guilt and pain he'd held inside for twenty long years.

Then the tears he'd banished came, unbidden, as if flushing away the lonely years and the unbearable fears, and Tommy could do nothing to stop them or the memories that washed over him like a warm, welcome wave.

Tommy closed his eyes for a moment, and then he opened them to watch the young lad walk across the expansive front yard toward him. Time seemed to still, then reel backward until Tommy saw not the grown-up adult version of his beloved grandson approaching him, but the little lad as he'd been the last time he'd seen him twenty years ago.

Tommy remembered he'd been coming around the front of the house from doing one chore or another late that afternoon when he'd heard the lad's happy squeals.

''Gwanpop.'' Jesse's laughter always brought a smile as the little lad scrambled across the front lawn on chubby legs that were not quite steady, racing from one misadventure to another. ''Gwanpop, save me,'' he'd plead, trying to contain his bubbling laughter.

''Come here, lad,'' Tommy would call, arms outstretched and a twinkle in his eye. Jesse would race to a stop, throw his chubby little arms up so his grandfather could lift him high in the air and out of harm's way.

''They're gonna get me.'' Jesse would giggle, snuggling closer to the safety and security of his grandfather's arms. ''Save me, Gwanpop. Save me!''

*They* were his older brothers, Jesse's consorts in crime, but aye, Jesse always knew where to go for reinforcements, always knew that his grandfather would rescue him, save him, protect him.

*Except for that one night when even his grandfather couldn't save him.*

Tommy's eyes opened and he blinked away his tears, blinking himself back to the present. *Dear God, the nightmare was finally, blissfully, over.*

With legs not quite steady, Tommy slowly started down the porch stairs, leaning heavily on his cane, never taking his eyes off the lad, fearing he might disappear in a puff of smoke.

Jesse watched Tommy approach, his heart pounding in a way that had nerves skimming just across his skin. He hadn't remembered his grandfather, hadn't remembered the ranch, his brothers, hadn't remembered anything.

At least not consciously.

Until his gaze met Tommy's.

The moment he'd stepped out of the rented SUV and seen Tommy Ryan standing on the porch, shadowed by the late-afternoon sun, silhouetted by the beautiful blue sky, Jesse knew in his heart—the only place it truly mattered—this *was* his grandfather.

His heart recognized him even if his mind or memory didn't. Jesse felt another chill race over him, followed quickly by a shiver that had him clenching his fists tightly.

Something deep inside him, in that place where there had always been this mysterious ache of longing and yearning, slowly seemed to fill.

He could only remember crying once in his life, when his mother passed on, but now he felt the quick burn of tears against his eyes, dampening his lashes. Jesse had to swallow, then clear his throat to speak.

''Grandpop.''

That one precious, welcoming word had the strength and energy draining from Tommy, had him blinking in joy, leaving his heart racing, his knees shaky.

''Aye, lad, 'tis me, Grandpop.'' Tommy's legs were so shaky he feared they wouldn't hold him up. He reached out his free hand toward Jesse, and for the first time in memory truly felt his age. His hand, gnarled now with age and arthritis, shook like a sapling in a storm.

''Jesse.'' His grandson's name came out a hoarse, broken sob as Tommy's knees buckled and he almost went down. Strong arms reached for him in much the same way he had once reached for, rescued and protected the young lad.

''Grandpop.'' Alarmed, Jesse caught his grandfather and held him in his arms. ''I'm here, Grandpop. It's okay, I'm here.'' Jesse simply held his grandfather, letting his eyes close and letting the emotions he'd tried to ignore all these months roll over him in a wave of love, loss and longing.

Shaken to the core, Tommy clung to his grandson. The lad's arms were strong and muscled, he thought proudly, letting his eyes close again. He just needed a minute, he told himself. Only a minute.

Tommy took a slow, deep breath to calm himself and the storm of memories and emotions marching wildly through him, shaking him to the core. His life in all its glory passed swiftly through his mind, and he knew in his heart of hearts this would be the crowning moment, the jewel of the joy in his wonderfully blessed life.

No man could ever want or need more.

Tilting his head back, Tommy's eyes opened and he looked into the blue eyes of his beloved grandson, unashamed of the tears that coursed down his cheeks.

"Aye, lad, how I've missed you." Tommy continued to cling to the lad's strength, needing to actually touch Jesse, to feel him, to know he was real. *This* moment was real and not just another dream where he'd awake disappointed and heartsick. Tommy wanted to savor every single second of this and bury it in his heart forever.

"I know, Grandpop." Jesse blinked back his own tears and held on to his grandfather tighter, not wanting to let him go just yet, feeling the enormous surge of love flowing from Tommy to him, leaving him awash in feelings so strong he wasn't certain his own legs would hold.

Lifting his head, Jesse let his gaze absorb his surroundings. They seemed achingly familiar, yet evoked no distinct memories.

At the moment he didn't need the actual memories. He had the feelings, and for now that was more than enough. Taking a deep breath, Jesse looked back down at his grandfather.

"Welcome home, lad," Tommy said with a brilliant smile that shimmered through tears. "Welcome home."

"Mama, why are you peeking out the window?" Riley asked, giving her grape Popsicle another lick, trying to catch a drip before it splattered on her top as she stood behind her mother in Tommy's kitchen.

Startled, Hannah gave a little shriek. The wooden spoon covered with remnants of the chocolate mousse she'd been making for the celebratory dinner this evening went flying, splattering bits of gooey chocolate all over the counter, the floor and a part of the wall.

"Riley." Whirling on her daughter, Hannah pressed a hand to her rampaging heart. "You scared the life out of me."

"I'm sorry, Mama," Riley said, taking another lick of her Popsicle. "But why were you peeking out the window?" Riley frowned. "You always said it wasn't polite to spy on people." Wide-eyed, Riley glanced up at her mother, intrigued. "Were you spying, Mama?" she asked, her eyes full of glee.

Hannah's face flamed beet red and she felt a hot flush wash over her face when she realized she'd been caught red-handed by her own daughter spying on Jesse Ryan!

Good Lord, what in the world had come over her? She was certain she'd never been so embarrassed in her life. Fine example she was setting for her little girl!

Blowing out a breath, Hannah shoved a loose pin back in her topknot and tried to figure out how to answer her daughter—honestly.

"Well...yes, and no, honey," Hannah said hesitantly, grabbing a paper towel and going down to eye level with Riley to wipe off her grape mustache. "I really wasn't...spying. I was...watching Uncle Jesse and Uncle Tommy. But I wasn't...spying. Definitely not spying, Riley.'' She forced a weak smile. ''That wouldn't be polite, right?''

''Right, Mama,'' Riley said with a grin.

The outright lie had Hannah's face flaming again. She *had* been spying on Jesse and Tommy since she and Riley had arrived at Tommy's house over an hour ago.

She hadn't seen or talked to Jesse or Tommy since she'd arrived; they'd been out walking around the ranch, talking, and she was nearly frantic, desperate to know how Jesse had handled the situation with Tommy, and more importantly, what he'd said to him.

Her heart was trembling with worry that Jesse might have hurt Tommy. And she couldn't deny that she was also concerned about Jesse and how the reunion with his grandfather had affected him.

She'd almost danced in relief when she caught sight of the two of them, arm in arm, walking back toward the large patio right outside the kitchen window. The window was closed, so she couldn't hear what they were saying, but at least she could see them now, sitting at the table, heads bent in quiet talk, or occasional laughter.

And her nerves had relaxed a bit when she saw the apparent camaraderie between the two men.

Until she looked at Jesse.

Then her nerves—her female nerves—the ones she'd ignored for so long began to squeal in feminine alarm just as they had this morning when she'd first seen him.

If only the man wasn't quite so darned attractive she might not be behaving like a lovelorn teenager, she thought in disgust.

"But how come you didn't just go outside and watch them?" Riley frowned, little golden eyebrows drawing together like a caterpillar across her forehead.

Good question, Hannah thought, watching as her daughter's tiny tongue, purple and sticky, took one final lick of the iced treat.

"Well, sweetheart, remember how I told you Jesse has just come home?" Hannah asked, removing the sloppy, wet purple stick from Riley's hand and tossing it into the trash.

"'Cuz he went away for a long time, right?" Riley swiped the back of her hand over her sticky mouth.

"That's right, honey." Hannah stood, grabbed another paper towel, dampened it, then took each of her daughter's hands and wiped them clean. "So, I thought it might be a good idea to let Uncle Tommy and Uncle Jesse have some time to talk alone." She gave her daughter's mouth a final swipe with the damp, and now purple, paper towel. "Do you understand?"

"I guess so, Mama," Riley said with a shrug, the confusion on her face clearly indicating she didn't quite understand. "But why were you watching them?"

With a smile, Hannah brushed a hand over Riley's head. "Well, honey, I love Uncle Tommy and I just want him to be happy."

"Don't you think Uncle Jesse will make him happy?" Riley asked with another frown, making Hannah realize she was only making the situation worse.

"No, honey. I'm sure Uncle Jesse is going to make Uncle Tommy very happy." She couldn't resist glancing over her shoulder to give another look at the two men, relieved to see them still deep in conversation.

"Mama, I'm bored," Riley said. "No one's here. And I don't know where they went. Even Ditka and Ruth are gone," Riley said with a frown and a barely suppressed yawn.

"Everyone should be home soon, honey." Hannah smiled as she glanced at the kitchen clock. She had less than two hours to finish an elaborate celebratory dinner. And that didn't include the time she needed to make her special chocolate mousse cake. It was Tommy's favorite. "Remember the note Uncle Tommy left for us?"

"The one you read to me, Mama?"

"Yes, honey. Uncle Tommy said he thought it would be best if he and Uncle Jesse had a chance to talk privately for a while, so he sent everyone out for the day." She pressed a hand to Riley's cheek as her precious daughter struggled to hide another yawn. "Everyone will be home for dinner. Remember we're having a big get-together tonight to celebrate Uncle Jesse coming home?"

"I 'member," Riley said, rubbing her eyes with a fist. "And Ditka and Ruth can come, too?" Riley asked, since she considered the dogs as much a part of the family as everyone else.

"Absolutely," Hannah confirmed with a smile. "But I think, sweetheart, that maybe you should take a little nap."

"But I'm not tired," Riley protested, moving her fist to rub her other eye.

"Oh I know, sweetheart," Hannah said, reaching for her daughter's hand. "I know. But if you don't take a nap, you might fall asleep and miss the celebration.

Now, you wouldn't want that, would you?'' Slowly, she began to lead her daughter out of the kitchen, toward the back of the house and the numerous guest bedrooms, bedrooms that Tommy insisted she or Riley use whenever they felt the need.

''No, I like celebrations,'' Riley admitted with a grin. ''Could we have cake and ice cream?''

Hannah laughed. ''I'm making your and Uncle Tommy's very favorite chocolate mousse cake right at the moment,'' Hannah said, leading her daughter into one of the bedrooms, decorated in pastel colors. She bent down and untied Riley's tennis shoes, then pulled the beautiful yellow comforter down, folding it neatly at the bottom of the bed. ''And we'll have vanilla ice cream as well.''

''Will Timmy and Terry be there, too, Mama?'' Yawning, Riley climbed onto the bed, slipping quickly under the cool sheets.

''Absolutely.'' Hannah bent and kissed her daughter's cheek. ''We couldn't have a celebration without Timmy and Terry, now, could we?''

''And can Matilda come, too, Mama?'' Riley snuggled deeper into the bed, her eyes drooping. ''She likes chocolate mousse cake and celebrations, too, Mama.''

Hannah laughed, trying not to shudder at the mention of Matilda, Timmy and Terry's pet tarantula. ''Yes, honey. Everyone will be there.'' Hannah kissed her daughter again. ''You sleep now, baby, and by the time you wake up, everyone should be home.'' Tiptoeing out of the room, Hannah closed the door with a smile and hurried back to the kitchen.

''Good Lord,'' she muttered when she saw the splattered spots of chocolate everywhere. Grabbing a damp cloth, she quickly wiped down the counters, the walls, then got down on her hands and knees to clean up the floor.

The snap of the back door shutting had her almost groaning. The last thing she wanted to have to do today was explain why she'd splattered chocolate over the previously spotless kitchen, especially when she was so busy and had so much to do.

When she saw the toes of the large Western boots right under her nose, she did groan.

"Darlin', what are you doing down there?" Jesse's deep voice was filled with concern. He reached for her hand, sending a shiver of awareness and nerves coursing through Hannah. "You shouldn't be down on your knees scrubbing floors," he said with a frown, helping her to her feet, trying to take the rag from her hand. "I thought you said you were a cook?"

Hannah brushed her damp, shaky hand over her white apron, hanging on to the rag with the other hand so Jesse wouldn't see how desperately his presence made her hands, and just about everything else, shake.

"I *am* a cook, Jesse," she insisted, rattled because he was so big, so masculine, and so intimidatingly gorgeous. How was she supposed to keep her composure when he set those laser-blue eyes on her, staring at her as if he could see straight into her heart and all the secrets she'd buried there? "It's just, I had a little accident," she said with a sheepish shrug.

Leaning against the counter, one eyebrow lifted in amusement as Jesse glanced at the floor and the few spots of chocolate she'd missed on the counter and walls.

"A chocolate accident is my guess," he said, unable to conceal the humor in his voice.

Hannah sighed. "Good guess," she admitted, trying to force herself to relax. "Jesse?" She dared to meet his gaze and felt her stomach tumble over.

"Yes, darlin'?" He surely enjoyed looking at her. She was dressed differently from this morning. Her hair was swept up in some kind of knot atop her head. But it was a little lopsided, and a few tendrils were rebelling, slipping free to frame her beautiful face. The shorts had been replaced by a pair of comfortable-looking jeans that hid those sinful legs. Pity, he thought, letting his gaze wander over the rest of her. He sure enjoyed looking at those long, gorgeous legs of hers. The white blouse she wore was covered by a large apron with a big red heart in the middle.

His gaze shifted, and for the first time he noticed her mouth. It was bow-shaped, with a sexy little indention right in the middle of her top lip. Devoid of color, they had something shiny on them, something that made a man ache to see if she tasted as good as she looked. His tongue suddenly itched to trace the outline of that sexy mouth. Slowly. Leisurely. Carefully. He shifted, diverting his thoughts to try to bring some relief to his suddenly tense body.

"Jesse, how did things go with Tommy?" She studied him, trying to read his face, his eyes, but the only thing she saw was amusement—and, if she wasn't mistaken, desire.

She wanted to flush again. She couldn't remember a

man ever looking at her that way before, at least not with such naked, blatant interest. Even though she might not ever have experienced it, it didn't mean she couldn't recognize it.

Or respond to it.

She could feel the heat of his gaze on her, feel it shimmer through her, evoking a heated response of her own.

"How'd it go?" Thoughtfully, Jesse crossed his arms across his chest, still thinking about that sexy little mouth of hers. Satisfied he'd have to taste that mouth—sooner or later—just to find out for himself, he turned and glanced out the window where Tommy was sitting at the patio table waiting for him. "About as well as could be expected, I guess," he said, turning back to her with a smile.

Swell, Hannah thought. He was just a fountain of information. "Is Tommy all right?" she asked nervously.

"All right, darlin'?" With a wry smile, Jesse shook his head. "You mean, have I done anything to warrant having you chase me around the kitchen with one of your frying pans?" He laughed at the look of horror that swept over her face. "No, darlin'. I promise I've done nothing to harm him or to warrant one of those pan-bashings." He lifted a hand to her cheek, unable to resist being so close and not touching her. It was something he could quite easily get accustomed to, he realized. "And I don't intend to do anything to harm him, Hannah. At least not intentionally."

"You know, you would have been fine had you stopped just a few seconds before," she admitted in irritation, chewing her bottom lip and resisting the urge to move her face so he wouldn't be touching her. It was hard to think with him so close, and his hands on her.

He laughed. "Well, darlin', I do believe we covered that this morning." He let his hand drop and cocked his head to look at her. "Remember?"

She nodded. "Yes, I remember," she admitted, blowing out a breath. "You don't make promises you can't keep."

"That's right." He started to reach out to her and was surprised when she reared back like a frightened filly. His eyebrows lifted. "Are you afraid of me, darlin'?" he asked quietly, stunned that he could have frightened this beautiful, incredible woman. He'd never frightened a woman in his life.

"Afraid?" Hannah repeated shakily, trying to ignore that his voice was like a soft, gentle caress, sliding over her and leaving her shaky. Her chin came up and Hannah struggled for pride. "Of course not, why on earth would I be afraid of you?" she asked indignantly, unwilling to admit that for the first time in her life she was afraid of what a man made her feel.

"Don't rightly know, now." He studied her for a moment, their gazes locked. Hannah watched as if in slow motion his hand lifted again and he gently brushed a finger down her cheek, then lifted it to his mouth.

Her eyes widened and it seemed as if everything inside her stilled as his mouth slowly opened, his tongue snaked out and he leisurely licked his finger.

The gesture was so blatantly sensual the pulse in her neck began to throb like a sore thumb.

"Grape," he finally said, a twinkle in his eye.

Hannah blinked, certain her temperature had jumped at least ten degrees. She had to swallow. Hard. "Ex...excuse me?"

"Grape." He showed her his finger. "You taste like grape." His deep voice was like a wave of warmth flowing over her, making her aware of every nerve in her body.

"Grape," she repeated dully. Her mind couldn't seem to register anything at the moment. She merely continued to stare at him. The amusement in his eyes finally forced her mind to kick in. "Oh, yes, I forgot." She managed a smile, trying to regain her composure. "Riley had a grape Popsicle." Hannah shrugged. "It dripped all over her." Hannah touched her cheek, not realizing it was sticky. "And apparently me as well."

Jesse glanced past her. "Well now, where is little Miss Riley?"

Hannah's grin was instant and she couldn't help but be touched by the fact that he thought enough to ask about her daughter. "Taking a nap. She wore herself out practicing on her new bike this morning." Following his lead, she crossed her arms across her breasts and leaned against the counter, grateful to have something to support her. "And she's been wandering around like a lost soul since we got here because everyone is out. I convinced her to take a nap so she could stay awake for the celebration tonight."

"Yes, the celebration," Jesse said with a sigh.

''You don't sound very happy about it.'' She watched him carefully.

''Happy?'' Jesse thought about it for a moment. ''Would you be happy knowing that you were going to meet about a dozen people you didn't know, or worse, couldn't remember, and yet be expected to act perfectly natural around?''

''Oh Jesse.'' Unconsciously she touched his arm to comfort him, her heart going out to him for the entire miserable situation. ''I can imagine how difficult this must be for you.''

''Not just me,'' he admitted, glancing back at Tommy again. ''It's got to be difficult for everyone concerned.'' He turned back to her and the wariness and pain in his eyes touched her heart.

She smiled at him, wanting to reassure him, to ease some of the wariness she saw in his eyes. ''Jesse, look, just try to take this one step at a time. There's no rush, really. You certainly can't make up twenty years in just a matter of hours or days. It's going to take some time.''

''Well now, darlin', time is the one thing I truly don't have,'' Jesse said, rubbing the back of his neck to ease a spot of tension that had settled there.

''What are you talking about, Jesse?'' Ignoring her own inner warning signals, she took a step closer to him, close enough that she could almost feel his body heat reach out and engulf her. She ignored it and focused on their conversation. ''What do you mean time is the one thing you don't have?''

''Well, darlin', I've got my own ranch to run back in Texas. And if you know anything about ranching, you gotta know that I can't be away from it for too long."

"You're not *staying?*" Her words edged upward in shock and bewilderment.

Jesse stared back at her with equal shock and bewilderment. "Stay?" He shook his head. "Now, darlin', why on earth would you ever think I was staying?"

Temper and frustration had her fists clenching again. "Because this is your *home,* Jesse!"

He shook his head. "You know, darlin', I do believe I'm growing to detest that little word."

"What word?" She glared at him, annoyed beyond belief. "What are you talking about?"

"Home, darlin'. Home." Rubbing his neck again because the tension had increased, Jesse shook his head. "I thought I explained all this to you this morning. Texas is my home. Has been for as long as I can remember."

"But what about Tommy?" she fairly cried. "What about your family?"

Jesse looked at her long and hard. "Well, darlin', I'm here now, aren't I? And for the moment that's all I can promise."

Her eyes slid closed and Hannah prayed her famous Irish temper wouldn't boil over. "Jesse," she began, choosing and spacing her words carefully. "How on earth can you simply turn your back on your family?" She shook her head, emotions spilling over. "My God, do you have any idea how lucky you are to even have a family? Let alone a family that is so welcoming and accepting, not to mention wonderful?"

He said nothing, he simply watched her, realizing that she was talking about a lot more than *his* family.

Something far more than her love and affection for Tommy and the Ryans was fueling this passionate display. Of that he was certain.

Watching her eyes light with fire and her cheeks flush with emotion, he felt two distinctly different emotions: the first was concern. Obviously someone had hurt her. The kind of hurt that remained deep in your heart and memories for a long time, coloring your emotions and your views. He suddenly wondered about Hannah's own family, and Riley's father as well.

The second emotion that caught him was pure unadulterated lust. And Jesse felt a hint of guilt for it, knowing that she was hurting. But any woman who was as obviously passionate as she was, was bound to be just as passionate in all areas of his life. And dang if it didn't just raise up all the wonderful possibilitics a passionate woman like her would bring to an encounter.

It was truly a shame he wasn't going to be here long enough to find out.

''How can you simply walk away from them?'' Hannah demanded, unable to even comprehend such a thing. In her entire life, the only thing she'd ever truly wanted was a family; a real family that would love and accept her. Jesse had one and he was simply turning his back on them. ''Don't you have any feelings?'' Biting back tears, she refused to allow him to see how upset she was. Refused to let him see that his mere words, his intended actions, had wounded her on a level she didn't feel comfortable or capable of dealing with at the moment.

Jesse pulled himself upright. "Hannah, darlin', listen to me." Gently, he took her by the shoulders, felt her trembling, then instinctively gathered her close, slipping his arms around her to press her against him. "Good Lord, darlin', you're so upset you're trembling." Concerned, Jesse gently caressed her back the way he might an injured foal. "It's not good for you to get yourself so riled up like this." He drew back to look at her, and caught her blinking back tears. "Truly, it's not."

Fists clenched against his chest, Hannah sniffled, trying to gather her composure. "Jesse." She glanced up at him and swallowed hard. He had the most incredible eyes. Every time she looked into them it made her feel things—want things—she knew better than to want or yearn for. That was a dream she'd given up years ago, and she wasn't about to let herself walk blindly down the path of misery and disappointment again. Not because of a man. "Does Tommy know you're not staying?"

"Well now, I must admit we really haven't gotten around to talking about that yet." He continued to caress her back, liking the feeling of having her in his arms. She was so small and delicate, and having her pressed against the length of him was causing his mind to come up with some incredibly imaginative fantasizing of what having that small, delicate *naked* body pressed against him might be like.

Caught up short by his own thoughts, Jesse shifted his weight so that all that was actually touching her was his arms. He knew better than to play with fire, and touching Hannah set off a fire he was more than certain would flame right out of control if he wasn't careful.

And he'd always been a careful, cautious man.

There was no point imagining or fantasizing about what could never be. She belonged here in Saddle Falls, Nevada. He belonged in Texas. He surely wasn't going to be around long enough to get involved with anything or anyone—especially a woman.

He couldn't, he reminded himself. He'd come to Saddle Falls only because of a deathbed promise, and he wasn't about to let himself get emotionally involved with anyone during the short time he planned to be here.

Not with Tommy.

Not with the rest of the Ryans.

And certainly not with Hannah.

He'd promised himself he'd stay detached and he would. Besides, it had never been a hardship before. He'd always had trouble forming attachments to people. It was the only thing about himself, about *Jesse Garland,* he'd never understood.

Until now, he'd never questioned his reserve, but simply accepted it as an inbred part of who he was.

When it came to emotional attachments, he simply balked and bailed. It was an action that had become a habit over so many years—with everyone, especially women. Perhaps that's why he'd never married. He'd come close once, but knew in his heart it wasn't right. He couldn't seem to allow his heart to let go of the reservations he felt; the invisible walls he'd built to keep people at bay. He simply couldn't allow himself to become emotionally attached. And so, not wanting to hurt the woman, he'd broken off the romance. After that, he made sure to keep all his relationships with women little more than superficial, not wanting to hurt anyone else. It had served him in good stead all these years and he wasn't about to change things now.

"Jesse, if you and Tommy haven't talked about how long you'll be staying—"

"You mean haven't talked about the fact that I'm *not* staying?"

"If you and Tommy haven't talked about the future, Jesse, do you think you might avoid talking about it? At least for a few days?" she added hurriedly at the look on his face. "I mean, why not give him a chance to just enjoy this time with you? He's waited so long to have you home again, I think it might be nice to give him a few days with nothing to worry or fret about."

"Well, darlin', I imagine I can do that." He touched her chin, forcing her to look at him. "I told you before, I'm not going to do anything deliberately to hurt him. Or anyone," he added softly. "It's not my way, Hannah. I've always prided myself on being an honorable man, and if you're worrying that I came here to hurt the Ryans or to stir up trouble, I do wish you'd put that thought out of your mind." It bothered him to know she thought so little of him and his intentions. Obviously her past history with men must have made her judge their characters poorly. "I don't intend to do anything of the kind."

She heaved a sigh of relief, desperately wanting to

believe him. "Then you won't discuss your plans with Tommy, at least not for a while?"

He grinned, chucking her under the chin. She looked utterly adorable with worry in her eyes and concerned words on her mouth. She was, he decided, one incredibly caring woman, a woman of deep loyalty as well as passionate emotion. Her intensity touched him profoundly and he couldn't help but admire her for it.

"Well, Hannah, I don't reckon anyone can say you're a pushover, now, can they?" He chuckled as her eyes lit with fire. "Now, don't go getting all riled, darlin'. I give you my word." He lifted his hand in the air as if taking an oath. "For the time being, I promise I won't tell Tommy I'm not staying. I promise not to discuss how long I'm staying. And I promise not to discuss the future or do anything deliberately to hurt Tommy, the Ryans or anyone else." His gaze searched hers. "I think that covers just about every eventuality, now, don't you think?" He continued to study her eyes, realizing there were emotions here he didn't reckon he understood. "Will that satisfy you, and remove those shadows of fear from those gorgeous eyes?" He slipped his hand from her chin, to stroke the silk of her cheek.

She was so close, and with her head tilted up like that, it put her luscious mouth right in his line of vision, making him ache.

For an instant, he wondered how Hannah would react if he dipped his head and pressed his lips to hers. Before he gave himself too much time to think about it, he decided to find out for himself.

"Hannah." Her name was a soft caress as he tilted

her chin farther upward and slowly lowered his head, his gaze never leaving hers. He saw the leap of fright in her eyes a moment before her hands pressed to his chest.

"Jesse." His name came out a husky whisper because her throat was so dry. "I...I..." She never had a chance to finish her thought. Never had a chance to tell him this was not a good idea.

Jesse's mouth, soft and coaxing, came down on hers, causing all thoughts to flee. She meant to push him away. She was sure of it. Instead, her hands slid from the broad expanse of his chest upward, to slide around him and cling.

She was certain the floor dipped, and then swayed, knocking her nearly off balance as Jesse's mouth gently seduced hers. Her heart began to knock a quick, staccato rhythm as he continued the kiss, keeping it soft, gentle and oh-so-tender. She reacted more to the tenderness than if he'd merely pressed his mouth against hers and kissed her senseless.

There was something more here, she realized, than a light flirtation. Something much more. She could feel it in his arms, in the way he responded, the way he held her, as if she was something to be treasured and cherished.

She'd never known the feeling and regretted it, regretted that she might never know it.

Until now.

And that's what scared her most. She'd yearned and longed to have a man treat her this way, as if she was special and important to him. And felt horribly guilty for her own selfish wanting.

But now, experiencing what she'd longed for all these years frightened Hannah simply because she knew it would not be easy to turn her back and walk away from the feelings.

But she knew she must.

For her sake. For his sake. And more importantly, for her daughter Riley's sake. She knew how disastrous letting her emotions cloud her judgment could be. Knew and had promised herself she'd never allow it again.

"Jesse." His name came out a husky whisper against his lips as Hannah savored the last moments of the kiss, then gently pulled back and away.

Heart hammering, she pushed her hair off her flushed face and forced herself to meet his gaze, praying he wouldn't know how much one kiss had affected her.

"That shouldn't have—we can't do that—" She shook her head, trying to put a thought together. It was difficult with him standing there studying her with those glorious blue eyes that seemed to see all the things she'd never wanted a man to be able to see. "I don't think this was a good idea." Unable to resist, she touched her trembling fingertips to her lips. They were warmed from his kiss, and she could still taste him there, which sent a wicked shiver of delight through her.

Jesse frowned, slipping his hands in his pockets so he wouldn't reach for her again. Kissing her was far more pleasurable than he'd even imagined. Too pleasurable. It was something he could clearly get used to very quickly. He clenched his fists in his pockets so he wouldn't reach for her again. Hannah surely packed a wallop. "Actually, darlin', I think it was a great idea." He grinned then, falling back into his customary role of keeping things light with women. But somehow with Hannah it seemed wrong. And he didn't quite understand why. "The best I've had all day, actually."

She shook her head. "No, Jesse, you have to understand something. I can't get involved with you."

"Something wrong with me?" he asked mildly, trying not to let male pride get in the way.

"No," she said quickly, too quickly. It had him grinning again. "Nothing's wrong with you, Jesse. It's just I can't get involved with any man."

"Don't like men?" he asked with a frown, almost laughing at the horror that flashed across her face.

"Of course not." Off balance, Hannah blew out a breath. "It's just that I don't have any room in my life for a man."

"I see. Unless I miss my guess, though, you must have been involved with a man at some point." At her questioning look he continued. "You have a daughter, Hannah, and unless you adopted her, and I doubt that since she's the mirror image of you, you were involved with a man at some point."

"Yes," she admitted hesitantly, not wanting to go into an explanation about her past. "But that was in the past." Stubbornly, she lifted her chin. "I...I... Jesse, it's just not feasible for me to get involved with you. Please understand?"

The fear and pleading in her eyes made him back off. He'd obviously been right about someone hurting her deeply, but he had a feeling today with everyone's emotions strung tight that it might not be the best time to get into it.

"Well, I don't reckon I can understand something you haven't clearly explained to me, but for the moment we'll let it go." At his words, her shoulders slumped in relief.

"Thank you," she said softly.

"You're welcome." He stepped back, dropping his arms to his sides. "Now, I came in here to rustle up something cool for Tommy and I to drink. Think you might be able to help me out with that?"

"Absolutely." Turning out of his arms, she reached over her head to open a cabinet and remove two glasses, deciding to ignore how shaken she was. "Tommy usually likes a glass of cold lemonade in the afternoon." She headed toward the fridge and pulled out the icy-cold pitcher of pink lemonade she'd just made. "If you'll hand me that tray sitting on the shelf up there." She pointed and he managed to reach it without the step stool she kept handy for just such occasions. She set the glasses and the pitcher on the tray, then scooted by Jesse to grab some white napkins from the counter before setting those on the tray as well.

"Would you like a snack or anything, Jesse? Are you hungry?"

He laughed, then shook his head as he took the tray from her. "No, darlin', but thanks for the offer." He cocked his head. "Are you really as good a cook as Tommy claims?"

"Absolutely," she said proudly, slipping her hands into her apron pockets. "And I'm sure during the next few days you can judge for yourself."

"I'm looking forward to it," he said, lifting the tray and heading toward the door.

"Jesse?"

"Yes, darlin', I know," he said with a chuckle. "Mind my step or you'll be measuring my head with one of your frying pans."

"Count on it," she said firmly, trying not to grin.

He stopped before going out the door. "And darlin', you remember I said we would drop the subject. *For the moment.*" He hesitated. "That doesn't mean we're not gonna pick it up again sometime soon."

The moment the back door closed behind him, Hannah gripped the counter tightly and pressed a hand to her heart, trying to gather her composure.

So many thoughts, feelings and emotions were rampaging through her, jumbling together in a confusing mix that had her more off base than she'd been in years.

She simply couldn't understand her physical or emotional reaction to Jesse. Granted, she knew now he wasn't the same Jesse she'd known as a child. He was a man now. A grown man. The kind of man that would make any woman's head spin.

She shouldn't allow herself to react to him like some silly, besotted schoolgirl. It was annoying and... exhilarating, she had to admit with a secret smile. It had been so long since she'd felt so alive simply because of a man's touch, his look, his smile, or even his kiss. So it was hard not to let caution go by the wayside and allow herself to just enjoy the feelings.

Hannah frowned, pushing another loose pin back in her hair. On the other hand, she knew better than to allow herself to be guided by her emotions. She knew better than anyone the consequences of letting them overrule her intellect and common sense.

And there was a lot more at stake here than just her own feelings. She was flirting with disaster, and she knew it. Jesse wasn't staying. He couldn't have been more clear about that. So why on earth would she allow herself to let her feelings get involved?

She couldn't and wouldn't, she told herself firmly, resolving to get a grip on herself.

Hannah lifted her head and glanced out the window. She couldn't help but smile at the joy on Tommy's face. She couldn't ever remember seeing that look in his eyes, and she knew Jesse was the reason.

But how was Tommy going to feel when he learned he'd found his grandson only to lose him again? Not by someone else's hand this time, but by Jesse's own rejection of his grandfather and his family.

Tommy was going to be devastated and she simply couldn't bear to see him hurt. She knew firsthand what it felt like to have your own family reject you, and she would do anything in her power to save Tommy or any of the Ryans from such a fate. It was a devastation that etched deep scars in your heart, scars that never fully healed.

Tommy had done so much for her and Riley, surely she could think of something to help repay him.

Her gaze shifted to Jesse and her heart tumbled over in spite of her own cautions. A thought began bubbling in her mind and she felt her spirits slowly lift.

She didn't have much time, but maybe, just maybe, she could show Jesse—teach Jesse—the importance of family. *His* family. She frowned suddenly, remembering another man she'd tried to teach the importance and value of family.

Hannah sighed, realizing regretfully that her own wounds still hadn't healed. Riley's father's deception and betrayal had left her so deeply wounded, so deeply disillusioned, that she wasn't certain she could ever trust another man who didn't or couldn't see the value and importance of family. Nor could she ever allow herself to fall in love with a man like that.

Like Jesse, she thought sadly.

But maybe it wasn't that Jesse didn't value family, maybe it was just that since he's never really had a family—at least not one he could remember—he didn't fully realize how wonderful being a part of a large, loving family could be.

Excited at the thought, Hannah's mind began to spin. Maybe if she could find a way to get Jesse to realize just how important family was, then he would realize that he belonged with *his* family. Right here in Saddle Falls.

Pushing away from the counter, Hannah decided it was certainly worth a try. She glanced out the window. At this point, she had nothing to lose.

And if it worked, she would have given Tommy the one thing—the only thing he'd ever really wanted—the return of his grandson to the family home and fold.

Just as Tommy had always given her the one thing she'd always needed and wanted—a family. A place where she belonged.

It was definitely worth a try.

## *Chapter Four*

"So, what do you think?" Hannah asked nervously as she put the finishing touches on the platter of prime rib she was preparing to carry into the dining room. Dinner was almost ready. Everyone had finally come home. Jake and his wife Rebecca who lived in a small carriage house behind the main ranch house. Josh and Emma who lived next door in the house Emma had inherited from her dad—while they built a new home of their own on the Ryan property. And Jared and his wife Natalie, who, along with their children lived in the main ranch house with Tommy.

The Ryan women had insisted on pitching in and helping to get dinner on the table, much to Hannah's relief. But then again, they never treated her like the help. Instead, they'd always included her and treated her like family.

Jake's wife, Rebecca, Jared's wife, Natalie, and Josh's wife, Emma, were just finishing setting the enormous dining-room table as well as a smaller table in the corner for the children.

With a wicked grin, Jesse leaned his hip against the kitchen counter, his gaze still on the Ryan women bustling around in the dining room. He glanced at Hannah, amused by the way her gaze had been following him all day. It felt kind of nice to know she was watching him. Although he wished it was out of personal interest rather than a desire to make sure he wasn't doing anything that would require her to grab one of her frying pans.

"Well, darlin', what I think is that the Ryan men certainly have great taste in women." He shook his head, his eyes twinkling in amusement. "They're all lookers, every one of them."

"True," she admitted, realizing he was both teasing her and trying to avoid the issue. Hannah swatted him with the pot holder she had in her hand, making him chuckle. Warmed from all the heat in the kitchen, she pushed back several loose strands of hair with the back of her hand and let her gaze meet his. "But that's not what I meant and you know it. How did it go with your brothers?"

Jesse shifted nervously, shifting his gaze to the living room where a football game was on and all the Ryan men—his brothers—were hooting and hollering and engaging in some good-natured arguing over what team was going to win.

He'd been sitting in there with them, enjoying the game, comfortable in spite of the circumstances. Almost by silent agreement, when everyone had returned to the house, men, wives, kids and dogs, no one had discussed anything heavy or asked any questions.

They'd merely greeted him with a handshake or a hug, sometimes both, and then basically let him be. And he appreciated that they were giving him time to adjust, time to feel comfortable. But Tommy had told him earlier during the day when they'd been sitting out on the patio that he'd asked everyone in the family to just let things develop at their own pace. Especially this first day.

And Jesse sorely appreciated it since he was still trying to struggle through all the emotions inside of him.

Including the emotions Hannah and her kiss had aroused.

When he realized that he'd rather be spending the few remaining minutes until dinner in the kitchen with Hannah he'd wandered in here.

"Things went as well as can be expected, I guess," he said with a shrug, turning back to Hannah and taking the heavy platter of meat from her hands. "This is too heavy for you to be lifting, Hannah," he said quietly. He'd been watching her all afternoon as well, finding excuses to go into the kitchen just so he could be with her. He'd been struck by how hard she worked.

But growing up with a single mother, Jesse knew how hard single mothers, especially those dedicated to their children, like Grace Garland and Hannah *had* to work. It was a complex juggling act. But still, he wondered and worried how Hannah did it. She had her job here, which was obviously very time-consuming and demanding, not to mention caring for Riley and that run-down monstrosity of a house they lived in. When he first came back into the kitchen, he'd realized just how frazzled Hannah looked from working all day.

"Let me carry this for you." Before she could protest, he started into the dining room. Hannah followed, knowing he was deliberately avoiding her question and the subject of his brothers. Why, she wasn't certain. But it made her nerves squeal in silent alarm since she'd been stuck in the kitchen when everyone came home, and she had no idea how that initial meeting had fared.

"Where would you like this?" Jesse asked, earning smiles from the assembled helpers.

"Just set it right in the middle of the table, Jesse," Hannah instructed as Emma reached across the table and moved the large, fresh floral arrangement Hannah had made for the celebratory dinner. Slender and petite, she had a cap of dark hair and large eyes that made her look fragile and delicate—but Emma was anything but.

"It looks fabulous, Hannah," Rebecca said with an envious sigh. She took a deep whiff, then pushed her long hair off her face. Rebecca still looked like the investigative reporter—pregnant or not. "And everything smells terrific."

"Thanks." In spite of the fact that she was used to compliments on her cooking, Hannah flushed with pride and pleasure.

"I keep telling Jake that I'm going to learn to cook—"

"Threatening me again, sweetheart?" Jake called

from the living room where he was sprawled deep in a chair with his baby daughter, Molly, nestled in his lap, sound asleep.

"No, Jake, just trying to expand my interests." Rebecca glanced at Jesse, feeling the need to explain. "My...uh...culinary expertise begins and ends with boiling hot dogs." She frowned a bit. "And of course, macaroni and cheese—the kind in the box," she hurriedly clarified with a laugh and a shrug. "Thank goodness I have a sister-in-law who owns a diner." She glanced affectionately at Emma, then at Hannah. "And Hannah for everything else. Otherwise Jake and I would probably starve."

"I didn't marry you for your cooking skills, sweetheart," Jake called, turning his head to wink at Jesse. "Trust me, bro, she has other more interesting...skills."

"Jake!" Appalled and embarrassed, Rebecca glared at her husband. "There are children here," she reminded him primly. "Including your own daughter."

"See what I mean?" Smiling at Jesse, Jake wiggled his eyebrows, amused by his wife's embarrassment.

"I reckon I do," Jesse said with a laugh, realizing he was enjoying the camaraderie as well as the company. With a grin, Jesse glanced at Rebecca. He'd liked her immediately, and the enormous love between her and Jake was obvious.

"You're almost as bad as he is," Rebecca accused with a roll of her eyes, making Jesse chuckle.

"Well then, darlin', guess that just means I'm falling behind." Still grinning, he slipped his hands in his pockets and sent Jake a wink. "Guess I'll have to work a bit harder, to catch up then."

"Men!" Rebecca said, aiming a napkin at Jesse, who ducked just in time.

"Hey, babe, the Ryan men stick together," Jake called back. His gaze met Jesse's and for a moment the two brothers, the oldest and the youngest, stared at each other, a silent message of understanding passing between them. Jesse felt something much stronger, deeper, pass through him, moving his heart in a way that left him shaken.

"You're all hopeless," Rebecca said with a laugh, earning a nod of agreement from her fellow Ryan females.

"Uncle Jesse's not hopeless," Riley defended indignantly, wrapping her arms around Jesse's leg and glancing up at him adoringly. "He's wonderful."

Chuckling softly, Jesse reached down and scooped Riley up in his arms. "Well now, darlin', thank you for defending my honor." He planted a loud, smacking kiss on her cheek and Riley snuggled closer. "I think you're wonderful too."

"See what I mean," Rebecca declared with a smile of pretend disgust, encompassing the rest of the women with a glance. "Five minutes and every female in the house adores him." She shook her head, then lifted her hands in supplication. "What on earth are we going to do with them?"

"Well, darlin'," Jesse said, a mischievous twinkle in his eyes as his gaze met Jake's and he saw the approval there, "I reckon between us we could uh...think of a few interesting things." Still holding Riley in his arms, Jesse turned toward Hannah. Their eyes met, held, and she couldn't help but think of the interesting kiss they'd shared. She flushed bright red and averted her gaze to the table. ''Yes indeed,'' Jesse said with a wink to Rebecca. ''*Very* interesting things.''

''Time to eat,'' Hannah all but groaned, anxious to be out from under Jesse's knowing gaze and charming smile.

Dinner at the Ryan household was always chaotic at best. On a night when the whole family had gathered, it was more like a three-ring circus, with kids spilling, giggling and teasing.

Adults passed overflowing platters of food back and forth, chattering one over the other, laughing and enjoying the company as well as the meal.

And through it all, Tommy Ryan sat at the head of the table, beaming at his family, totally content.

''Tis a glorious night for a celebration,'' he finally said when dinner had been completed and Hannah's decadent chocolate mousse cake had been oohed and aahed over and devoured.

Now, as coffee was passed and after-dinner drinks poured, Tommy wanted a moment to savor this night, this dinner. And his family.

He lifted his brandy snifter, then let his gaze travel around the table. His heart warmed and swelled until he felt for certain it would burst from the joy filling it to nearly overflowing.

He cleared his throat to get everyone's attention. The din softened but didn't silence until he picked up his knife and tapped it gently against the delicate snifter he held in his hand. The room quieted instantly and all eyes turned to him.

"The entire Ryan clan is gathered together tonight for the first time in twenty years." Pride had him swallowing the lump that had clogged his throat as he let his gaze shift around the table. "And what better time for a toast?"

"To my eldest grandson, Jake." He smiled as a rumble of laughter worked around the table. "Aye, I must admit you were always a rebel and a hellion, truth be told. And you gave me more than your fair share of worry." Tommy's own chuckle mixed with everyone else's. "More so than all your brothers combined. But I'm pleased to say you've grown into a fine, fine man, Jake. Tamed, of course, by the right woman." Tommy tipped his glass in salute toward Rebecca, who blew him a kiss in return. "And I'm proud of you, Jake. Very proud. You and Rebecca have given me a beautiful granddaughter, a lass who I'm certain, with the true luck of the Irish, will grow up to give you back all the worry that you gave to me." Amidst laughter, Tommy lifted his glass, as did everyone else, and took a sip of his brandy before continuing.

"Then there's Jared." The murmurs were as quiet and subdued as the man himself. Tommy shook his head. "Aye, son, you were always more like your father than any of your brothers." Tommy's voice had softened a bit at the mention of his long-deceased son, the pain still raw after all these years. "Looking at you, lad, why, it's like looking at your father when he was a young man. All quiet strength and solemn responsibility. You worried me some, too, if the truth be told—''

''Me?'' Jared said in surprise, ignoring the laughter that rippled around the table. As the second oldest, Jared had the same dark hair and enormous Ryan blue eyes but he was much more serious and subdued than his brothers.

''Aye, lad, you,'' Tommy admitted with a twinkle in his eyes. ''You were far too serious for your own good. Your love of the land—Ryan land—made me worry that you'd never find it in your heart to love anything else.'' Tommy's gaze shifted to Natalie, Jared's wife who reached for her husband's hand under the table. With her long ebony hair and slender figure, it was hard to believe she was the mother of four. ''But, aye, like your oldest brother, you were fortunate to have the love of a good woman to help you see the light, to show you there was more to life than...cow patties.'' Laughter swelled again and Tommy paused, waiting for it to quiet down. ''And you're well on your way to having a full-scale clan of your own.'' Grinning, Tommy tipped his glass to the corner of the dining room where four bassinets, two holding Jared's infant twin sons, were lined up and where a small table had been set for the children.

The table was empty.

Timmy and Terry, Jared and Natalie's oldest set of twin boys were too busy trying to feed gumdrops to the dogs, Ruth and Ditka, *under* the table to notice that all eyes were on them.

Tommy chuckled as he returned his attention to Jared once again. ''And lad, I couldn't be prouder.''

Lifting his glass, Tommy took a sip, then added. "May you be blessed with a dozen more sons, lad, twins all of them."

At Jared's groan, everyone laughed as Tommy continued.

"Now then there's Josh," Tommy said with a deliberately heavy sigh, making everyone chuckle again. "Aye, with your fancy business and law degrees, you've always had a head for business and you've secured the Ryans' future—all the Ryans—" Tommy inserted, letting his gaze encompass everyone, adult and child alike. "For all of our futures." Bringing his gaze back to Josh, Tommy grinned. "And lad, I couldn't be prouder." Tommy shook his head. "But aye, along with that head for business, lad, you also had an eye...for the ladies." Josh grinned until his wife, Emma, gave him a delicate poke with her elbow. It was a rare day when Josh, who was the spitting image of his brothers, wasn't dressed in his usual businessman's suit—and today was one of those days making Josh look less like a tycoon and more human and approachable. "You gave me a spot of worry, too, lad, wondering if the only thing you'd every let claim your heart was the next deal." Fingering his glass of brandy, Tommy glanced up at Emma, then grinned broadly, love shining in his eyes. "But, like your brothers, you're no fool. You knew a good woman—the right woman—when you saw her—"

"Yeah, even if it did almost take a steamroller to hit him before he realized it," Jake said, resting his arm over the back of his chair as he winked at Emma and then grinned at his brother Josh.

''And now, lad, you and Emma have given your late grandmother a namesake, little Brie,'' Tommy said, letting his gaze shift to one of the white bassinets where his youngest granddaughter lay sleeping quietly. At least for the moment. ''Aye, lad, she would have been proud, your grandmother. Very proud. As am I.'' Tommy lifted his glass again and took another sip before turning his attention to Jesse.

He stilled for a moment, gathering his thoughts. When he spoke again, his voice was shaking with emotion. The table quieted as all eyes turned to him.

''Jesse.'' Tommy paused, trying to contain the wild rush of emotion, lifting his gaze to Jesse's, seeing so many, many things in the lad's face.

Sitting opposite Tommy, at the other end of the table, Jesse shifted his weight nervously, unaccustomed to being the center of attention. Especially in a room full of so many people—virtual strangers, his mind corrected. But he didn't feel uncomfortable, he realized. Just a small bout of nervousness, which he figured was only natural.

Under the table, he felt Hannah reach for his hand. She'd been sitting next to him all during dinner. Every once in a while he'd sneak a glance at her, or catch her looking at him. They'd both quickly look away, as if embarrassed to be caught looking at the other. It both amused and intrigued him.

Now, feeling the warmth of her hand on his made him relax just a bit more, certain he could endure whatever was to come, feeling just a bit more comfortable than he had several hours ago, realizing *she* had a lot to do with it.

In spite of her dire warnings about what would happen if he hurt Tommy or any of the Ryans, he felt as if she was his special ally who would be there if she needed him. There was some kind of deep emotional connection between them, Jesse realized. And he didn't understand it any more than he'd understood anything else during the past three months. All he knew was that it was there between them, drawing them closer in a way he found natural. Comfortable.

It had been a long time since he'd felt so comfortable with a woman, Jesse realized. A long time. And longer still since he hadn't run when a woman had touched something deeper than his body. But there was no denying Hannah had.

It scared him, admittedly, but he wasn't running yet, he thought. He couldn't. So he'd just have to be careful, he realized. Mind his step, as she would say. Because the last thing he wanted to do was lose his heart. He'd already lost so much, he didn't want to add anything else to the mix, especially since his emotions were both raw and torn now, making it far too easy for him to let his feelings go unchecked.

Something he knew he had to be careful of.

He glanced at her now, amazed again at how beautiful she was. Even after a day spent in the kitchen, bent over a hot stove cooking. He smiled at her, enjoying her touch, her warmth.

He squeezed Hannah's hand in acknowledgment, then linked his fingers through hers and held on, wondering how she kept her hands so soft when she worked as hard as she did.

"Jesse, my boy," Tommy began. "It's been a very,

very long time since you sat at this table with your family.''

''Too long,'' Jake interjected, meeting his baby brother's gaze.

''Hear. Hear,'' Josh said, lifting his glass with a hand that wasn't quite steady to take a sip of his drink.

''We've missed you more than words can ever say,'' Tommy continued softly, never letting his gaze waver from Jesse's. ''There was a time we thought we'd never have this night together.'' Tommy's smile was small and he had to take a sip of his drink to clear his throat again.

''A long time,'' Jared said quietly, reaching out an arm to catch his son Terry and to slow him down a bit before he raced off after the dogs.

Tommy smiled across the table. ''But you're here now, lad, and we couldn't be happier. 'Tis a dream come true for the Ryans. All the Ryans,'' Tommy emphasized. ''And although there have been many years passed, and many memories lost, we all want you to know how proud we are of you, and how happy we are that you're home.'' Tommy's voice broke and he shook his head as he reached in his pocket for his handkerchief to dab his eyes. With a sniffle and a smile, he lifted his glass in the air. ''To you, Jesse, my boy. Welcome back to the clan.''

''Hear, hear.'' Glasses were raised in toast, and Hannah found herself watching Jesse, feeling a surge of warmth for him. He'd been nothing but a gentlemen with his family all day. Whatever she'd been expecting hadn't come to pass. For the moment at least, Jesse seemed to be handling everything just fine.

Her gaze shifted to Tommy. And dear, sweet Tommy couldn't be happier, she thought, knowing Jesse had been the cause.

She glanced back at Jesse again and found him watching her curiously. She flushed a bit, trying to free her hand from his. But he held on, lifting it from under the table, in full view of everyone, before lifting her hand to kiss.

"That was a wonderful meal, Hannah," he said quietly. "Thank you."

"Aye, lass, a thousand pardons," Tommy said with a shake of his head. "I must be getting daft in my old age, to not even mention this fine, fine meal you prepared for us." With a grin, Tommy lifted his glass to her. "To Hannah. We don't know what we'd do without you."

"Starve," Jake said, earning a poke in the belly from Rebecca and laughter from everyone else.

Tommy waited for the table to quiet before continuing, his gaze firmly on Hannah's. "Lass, you know I was never blessed with a daughter, but aye, you've been the daughter of my heart. You're a welcome addition to this family, and a well-loved one at that."

"Oh, Tommy." Tears in her eyes, Hannah pressed her free hand to her lips. "I love all of you as well."

"May you find all the happiness you want and deserve. And be blessed with a dozen more little lasses like your darling Riley."

Hannah almost choked at the thought. "A dozen?" she laughed. "I think I'd better settle for the one indignant imp I've got."

"To you both, then, Hannah. With our love and appreciation.'' Tommy lifted his glass toward her and drank deeply, letting his gaze go around the table at his family one more time, feeling a peace and contentment that had eluded him for many years.

''You truly love them, don't you?'' Jesse whispered to Hannah. She turned to him. He was still holding her hand, and her heart and pulse were reacting in kind.

''Yes,'' she admitted with a small smile. ''More than I can ever say.'' She met his gaze, held it. ''They're my family,'' she said simply. ''They always have been and always will be.'' She hesitated a minute. ''They're yours, too, Jesse,'' she said quietly, holding his hand tightly. ''If you'll let them be.''

Jesse said nothing. Instead, he raised her hand, kissed it gently, then glanced away, leaving Hannah with an odd ache in her heart.

''Uncle Jesse, I'm *really* glad you came home,'' Riley said, snuggling deeper into his lap with a huge yawn. Night had fallen, the dinner table had been cleared, and dishes were done. Now a hint of moonlight filtered in through the Ryan living-room windows, casting a warm, sweet glow throughout.

''You are, darlin'?'' He grinned at her. ''Now why's that?''

''Well...'' She hesitated, then glanced around the Ryan living room where everyone was engaged in some after-dinner relaxation. She lowered her voice to a conspiratorial whisper. ''Because Timmy and Terry gots a daddy who plays with them and holds them on his lap.''

Jesse glanced at Jared, sitting with his arm around

his wife, Natalie, as they each held a twin—little Jesse, also known as J.J. to avoid confusion, and Joey—who were only a few months old.

Jesse's gaze shifted, watching in amusement as Timmy and Terry, Jared and Natalie's older twins, sat at their parents' feet, surreptitiously trying to feed the dogs more gumdrops. Jesse had to smother a laugh. He had to give Jared and his wife credit. It took a great deal of guts to handle two sets of twin boys. He loved children and looked forward to having them, but he wasn't certain he was quite *that* brave.

"Yes, darlin'," Jesse said, turning back to Riley who shifted and slung one arm possessively around his neck. "I can see that."

"And...even little Molly gets to sit on Uncle Jake's lap." It was hard not to miss the longing in the little imp's voice.

Jesse glanced across the room. Jake was holding his baby daughter in his lap, bouncing and cooing at her, all the while keeping up a heated debate with his wife, Rebecca, about the name as well as the sex of their next child.

Rebecca had assured everyone at dinner that she hadn't conceived yet, but didn't want to wait to the last minute. She was convinced another girl was in the offing, while Jake was certain this time it had to be a boy.

"I can see that, too, darlin'," Jesse admitted, realizing with a pang where this was going. Oh, what this child was doing to his heart, he thought, tying a rope around it and lassoing it for sure.

"And Uncle Josh or Aunt Emma are always holding or playing with Brie," Riley added with a huge sigh that sounded far too much like longing, a longing that deeply touched Jesse's heart.

His gaze shifted again, following Riley's line of vision to where Josh and his wife, Emma, sat snuggled together on a love seat, their daughter, Brie, quietly sleeping on her father's shoulder.

"Well, darlin'," Jesse began, realizing Riley had laid her head on his shoulder and was struggling to stay awake. "I imagine it's because Brie's just a little tyke. And I don't reckon she can sit up by herself yet. So that's why she has to sit on her mama or daddy's lap."

"Sometimes I get to sit on one of their laps but not always." Eyes drooping with fatigue, Riley managed a smile as she wound her skinny arm tighter around Jesse's neck and snuggled into a more comfortable position. "But now that you're here, Uncle Jesse, I get to sit on your lap."

"Why, you're absolutely right, Miss Riley," he said quietly, touched by the openness and vulnerability in the child. "Seeing's how I don't have any babies of my own to keep my lap warm, I guess you're gonna just have to do the job for me." Grinning at the delight on her face, he pressed his forehead to hers. "That is, if you don't mind?"

She shook her head furiously, sending her pigtails flying. "I don't mind, Uncle Jesse." Her head continued to shake. "Honest. I like sitting on your lap."

"Well now, darlin', I like having you sit here." He jiggled his leg, bouncing her a bit as she snuggled even closer to him.

"Jesse." He felt Hannah's hand on his shoulder and

turned to her with a smile. "I think I'd better take her home. She's almost asleep on her feet."

"I'm not tired, Mama," Riley protested, hugging Jesse tighter.

"Yes, sweetheart," Hannah said, running a gentle hand over her daughter's head. "I can see that you're not tired," she said, giving Jesse a meaningful glance.

Every time she saw Jesse with her daughter, saw the patience and love flowing from him, Hannah was torn between wanting to weep and wanting to jump for joy.

Weep because of all that Riley had missed by not having a father of her own. A father that, as Riley grew older, would be missed more and more. And the thought of depriving her daughter of something—anything—she wanted and needed so desperately made Hannah infinitely sad.

Long ago, she'd realized she could give her daughter all her love, all her attention and devotion, but she couldn't give her a father, and Hannah *wouldn't* give Riley a father who didn't want her or couldn't accept her. No, Hannah thought. It was much better this way. Much better. Never knowing her father was better than having to try to accept the fact that her father didn't want her, Hannah realized from her own personal experience. And although she might not be able to provide a father for her daughter, she could protect her child in the best way she knew how. And for now, that would just have to be enough.

But every time she saw Jesse with her daughter, saw his kindness, his patience and his simple goodwill toward her, it brought both an ache to her heart as well as a round of joy. There were very few men in the world who would treat a child the way Jesse had treated Riley from the moment they'd met.

Jesse gave Riley his undivided attention, making it quite clear he had a genuine affection for children. He seemed to understand them on a level most adults didn't.

He didn't patronize Riley, nor did he try to pacify her. He merely treated her with respect and dignity, like a person, and not a child. Something that was very rare and very hard for most adults to do.

"Hannah, if you want, Jared can run you and Riley home," Natalie offered, carrying a sleeping baby of her own toward his bedroom.

"Thanks, Natalie," Jesse responded, standing and cradling Riley in his arms. "But if it's all right, I think I'll walk them home."

"Fine by me," Natalie said as she headed down the hallway toward the twins' bedroom.

"Jesse." Hannah placed a hand on his arm. "That's not necessary. Jared can drive us, or I can walk by myself." She smiled at him. "Riley and I walk home all the time." She shrugged. "It's really no big deal. It's been a long day and I'm sure you're tired."

"Not too tired to walk my best girl home," he said, planting a soft kiss on Riley's head. He glanced down at her, noted her eyes were closed and there was a look of happy contentment on her face. It pleased him on a level too deep for him to understand at the moment. "Go get your things," he instructed Hannah. "I'll meet you out front." After explaining that he'd be back in a little bit, Jesse headed out the front door with Riley in his arms.

The night had barely cooled off, but the sky was clear and almost a pearly black, with stars twinkling overhead like diamonds set on fire.

"It's beautiful, isn't it?" Hannah asked, coming out the front door and down the steps to join him. She lived across the street and less than a block away.

"That it is, darlin'," he admitted as they started walking toward the hill. Deliberately, he slowed his steps to match hers. He glanced at her, worry etched on his face. "You look beat."

She smiled, then shook her head. "I guess I am a little tired. But it's been a long and extraordinary day," she admitted, giving him a smile. "But tomorrow's my day off, so I'll have a chance to rest a bit and get caught up."

"So tell me, what do you do on your day off?"

She laughed, reaching in the back pocket of her jeans for her house keys. "Well, the question might be what don't I do?" She shook her head, inhaling long and deep of the fresh night air. It felt good after being cooped up inside all day. "Let's see, tomorrow I'll go on spider patrol."

"Spider patrol?" he repeated with a lift of his eyebrow, making her laugh. "And what exactly is spider patrol?"

"Well," she began thoughtfully, "this is the desert, Jesse, and we have lots of creepy-crawly things. Particularly spiders. Black widows. Scorpions and tarantulas. Now, I'm not a coward, but I'm also not partial to creepy things." She grinned at him. "They give me the creeps," she laughed, rubbing her hands up and down her arms at the thought. "They also make me screech and squeal like a hyena,'' she admitted. ''Not to mention that if Riley even sees one she has nightmares for weeks.'' She paused to take a deep breath. ''So once a month, at night, I go on spider patrol. I take a flashlight and go out into the backyard—accompanied by the largest, meanest-looking stick I can find, and using my flashlight I find the spiderwebs. Wherever they've made their webs are where the babies are—''

''And babies grow up to be big, right?'' he asked, understanding completely.

''Absolutely. So, as long as I find and destroy the webs it keeps the spider population under control.''

''Do you do this every month?'' he asked in surprise, realizing that in spite of her lighthearted recitation, this was clearly something she didn't find particularly pleasant. But she was doing it for her daughter, he thought, feeling another burst of admiration for her. Overcoming her own fears to protect her child.

''At least,'' she admitted. ''No matter how late or how tired I am. I try to do it no less than every month.'' She shrugged. ''And I'm about due. I particularly want to do it now. The last thing I want along with all of Riley's other fears about school is for her to see a spider and then start having nightmares.''

''I see,'' he said quietly. ''Okay, so what else do you do on your day off?''

''Well, I have to cram a lot into tomorrow, Jesse. But just because the next few weeks are going to be very hectic. I have to go grocery shopping for my own house. Then it'll be a trip to the doctor with Riley to get her final checkup before she starts school.'' Hannah shook her head. "It's hard to believe she's going to start school in less than two weeks." She glanced affectionately at her daughter who was sleeping soundly in Jesse's arms. "She's growing up so fast," Hannah said wistfully, feeling a tug in her heart.

She'd always known Riley would probably be her only child, and she'd thought she'd come to accept it. But knowing she'd never be able to have the big family she'd always desired and yearned for made her sad.

Being a mother had always been the most important, wonderful thing she'd ever done, and she loved it.

Still looking wistfully at her daughter, Hannah sighed, wishing things could be different for her, wishing for all the other things women her age wanted, like more children. A husband. A real family. Someone to lean on during tough times; someone to share things with during good times.

Surprised by her own thoughts, Hannah quickly shook the notion away. She certainly didn't have time for self-pity or regrets. She had a beautiful daughter, a wonderful job and a very nice life. It should be more than enough.

"Riley and I will make a quick stop at the library to return some books and pick up new ones so I can read to her every night. Then we'll hit the mall for some last-minute shopping for school clothes and a new pair of tennis shoes for her, and then it's back home to do some chores around the house before dinner."

Amazed, Jesse shook his head as they neared her house. "And that's what you call a day off?"

She laughed. "Absolutely."

They were standing in front of her house now. Jesse glanced up at the imposing white structure, now faded and forlorn. "Are you telling me you maintain this house all by yourself?"

She laughed, heading up the back-porch steps to unlock the door. When she hit the third step, it gave a long, ominous creak. "Either I do it, Jesse, or it doesn't get done." Hannah glanced at the house she'd grown up in. It wasn't until she'd had Riley, a child of her own, that she'd actually starting thinking of this house as a home. Perhaps because it never had been before. She'd grown up in this house and had returned to Saddle Falls when she got pregnant, renting a small apartment in town. After her parents' deaths when she learned they'd left the house to Riley in trust, Hannah had moved back to her childhood home with her own daughter, determined to make it a *real* home. "Do you mind carrying her up to bed?" Hannah whispered as she swung open the door and stepped into the darkness of the mudroom. Quickly, she flipped on a light, then led Jesse through the house and up the stairs.

"Her bedroom is right there, at the end of the hall." Walking ahead of him, Hannah was already pulling stuffed animals and dolls off the bed when Jesse laid Riley down.

"Uncle Jesse?" Riley whispered sleepily as her mother pulled off her tennis shoes and set them on the floor.

"Yes, darlin'?" He sat down on the bed next to her, brushing her hair out of her eyes. Gently, he reached up and freed her hair from their pigtails.

"Can you come over to play tomorrow?"

Smothering a smile, Jesse glanced up at Hannah. ''Well, darlin', your mama seems to have a full day planned. I don't reckon she's going to have time to...uh...play with me what with spider patrol, shopping and going to the doctor.''

''Please?'' The pleading in the child's eyes caught his heart. Riley managed to lift herself on one elbow and motioned him closer with one finger. ''Mama's afraid of spiders,'' she whispered.

''Is that a fact?'' Jesse said.

Riley nodded sleepily. ''They make her screech and run.''

Banking a smile at the image, Jesse tucked the blanket up higher on Riley. ''Well then, darlin', I reckon I'd best better come over then, don't you think? We sure don't want your mama screeching and running, now, do we?'' he whispered, making the child giggle. ''Why, she just might scare those spiders to death.''

Still giggling, Riley scrunched her pillow, making it more comfortable before snuggling down on it. ''Could you go shopping with us, too, Uncle Jesse? I'm getting new clothes for school.'' She yawned, snuggled deeper under the covers. ''I'm not afraid to go to school,'' she said sleepily. ''Honest, Uncle Jesse. Some kids will be scared, but not me.''

''Of course you're not scared, darlin'.'' The tugs on his heart were a pleasant surprise, as was the fierce sense of protectiveness that rose up. Charmed, he pressed a kiss to her forehead. ''And I'd love to go shopping with you, Miss Riley. Provided that you promise to go to sleep now.'' He slid his finger down her nose. "Didn't anyone ever tell you sleep makes you beautiful?"

"'kay, Uncle Jesse." She yawned. "Good night."

"Night, darlin'." Jesse kissed her forehead, then rose, and waited in the hall while Hannah tucked her daughter in, gave her a good-night kiss and snapped the light off. Hannah took one long look at her sleeping daughter before shutting the door softly behind her.

When she turned he was right there, blocking her path, his eyes on hers. Suddenly nervous, Hannah wrung her hands together. "You know, Jesse, you're very good with her."

He shrugged off the compliment. "She's adorable. It would be hard not to be." He touched Hannah's cheek. She looked beat; her eyes were shadowed and her shoulders looked tight. He wanted to reach out and massage the tension from those beautiful slender shoulders. Instead, he tucked his hands in his pocket, remembering his own cautions to himself. "You've done an incredible job with her. She's an absolute pistol of a kid."

Pleased at his words, Hannah laughed, realizing they were standing in the quiet, empty hallway, bathed in the very dim light of the hall night-light, which created an unusual sense of intimacy.

She was trying not to be nervous. But she knew how she responded to Jesse, his touch and his mere presence. Right now, she was tired, her nerves taut from the long, emotional day, and her defenses were not where they should be. So why wasn't she more on guard? she wondered, looking up at him. She didn't know, and that frightened her far more than anything else. She rarely let her guard down with a man.

"Would you like some coffee?" she asked, trying to move past him. Ignoring his own mental cautions, he blocked her path, sliding his hands to her waist and holding her in place. The look in his eye and the grin on his face had her backing up a bit, until she felt the wall at her back. Her pulse kicked up a notch and she could feel it thumping pleasantly in her ears.

"Actually, darlin', there is something I want." His smile was slow, sexy and lethal as his gaze settled on her mouth, and he stepped closer, close enough to her to feel the warmth of his body run the length of her. "But it sure isn't coffee."

## *Chapter Five*

"Jesse." Hannah had to swallow. The look on his face, in his eyes, was wreaking havoc on her defenses. And she was far too tired at the moment to truly fight off the feelings swamping her. Her defenses were depleted by sheer nerves and adrenaline, not to mention a full day of work. "I told you, I don't think this... is...uh...a good idea."

Surprised by the panic that leaped in her eyes, Jesse decided to back off. The last thing in the world he wanted was to scare her or make her uncomfortable.

One brow rose. "I was just going to ask you what you do for fun." The twinkle in his eye set her face flaming.

"Oh!" Hannah shook her head, feeling horrifically embarrassed. "I'm sorry, I—"

"Yeah, darlin', I know." He grinned at her. "But

seems to me you're about dead on your feet and you don't need to be pushed or pressed any further today.'' He shrugged. ''I just wanted to know what you do for fun.''

She laughed, dragging a hand through her hair. He surprised her by reaching up and tugging the pins loose, letting her hair spill free down her back, then combing his fingers through the silky strands. Even though he only touched just her hair, she could feel the quick increase in her pulse from his nearness.

''Fun?'' She wasn't going to be able to think, let alone talk, if he kept touching her. It muddled her mind, she realized. Simply muddled her mind. Something that had never happened to her before.

''Yeah, you do know what fun is, don't you, darlin'?''

Her mind went blank and she stared at him for a moment. ''Jesse, I have to be honest. I can't remember the last time I did anything just for fun.''

One eyebrow rose, but he wasn't particularly surprised. Her plate was filled with responsibilities, leaving very little time for recreation. ''Well, Hannah, seems to me that's something we need to correct.''

As long as he was planning on being here for a few days, he'd decided he wanted to spend that time getting to know her—and Riley—a bit better. There was no harm in that, he assured himself. As long as he remembered this wasn't permanent. This wasn't serious. This was merely one old friend getting reacquainted with another.

''Correct?'' She frowned. ''Jesse, I don't know—''

''Turn around,'' he whispered softly.

She blinked in confusion. "Excuse me?"

"Turn around, darlin'." Taking her by the shoulders, he gently turned her so her back was facing him. "Now, I want you to take a long, deep breath and then let it out very slowly." He began to knead and massage her tight shoulders as she did so, pressing against the spots of tension until there was a low, soft purring in her throat, a sound that was incredibly arousing to him.

"Oh, Jesse," she moaned, letting her head fall forward. "If this is your idea of fun, I think I'm going to like it."

He laughed, and continued kneading, realizing he liked touching her, liked the way her body responded to him, liked the way her voice was husky deep in her throat. In another time and place, that purr would be highly erotic, he thought, shifting his weight to relieve the pressure his own body was feeling.

Sliding his fingers upward, he massaged the base of her neck and into her hairline, using his fingers in a circular motion until he could all but feel the tension seep from her.

"Feel better?" he murmured against her ear. The urge to trace the outline of that ear with his tongue was nearly overwhelming, but he resisted.

Hannah shivered. He was so close, she could feel the whispering warmth of his breath against her neck and her ear and it sent a wicked tremor of longing and need through her.

"Much," she murmured, allowing herself to relax and lean back against him. She could feel the hard length of him pressed against her back. Her softness nestled comfortably against his male hardness. Her face flamed a bit when she realized that he was just as affected as she was by the touch of their bodies.

"Good." Deciding he'd better quit before he did something he'd regret, Jesse planted a soft kiss on her neck, felt a quick shiver jolt her, then turned her by the shoulders to face him again. "Now, go take a long, hot bubble bath and get some sleep." He kissed her forehead, not trusting himself or his body to do any more. "And I'll see you tomorrow."

She nodded, still trying to regain control of her traitorous body. An impossibility whenever he seemed to be around, close enough to smell, to touch.

"Jesse, listen." She laid her hands to his chest. "I know Riley asked you to come over tomorrow, but I'm sure there are a lot of things you have planned. So I don't want you to feel obligated to her. I'll just explain tomorrow that you're busy."

"Darlin'." He shook his head. "I told you something before—several times as I recall—but apparently you didn't believe me." His gaze met hers as he lifted her chin so she had no choice but to look at him. "I never make promises I can't keep. And I would never make a promise to a child I wasn't about to keep. Definitely not my style, darlin'." He grinned at the relief that passed over her face. "Now, I'll see you *and* Riley tomorrow." He chucked her under the chin. "Go take your bubble bath, then go to bed. I'll see myself out."

Watching him walk down the hall and down the stairs, Hannah had to rub her hands over her arms. She wasn't chilled. No…what she was feeling was far more complicated.

When she heard the back door click shut, she leaned

against the wall and closed her eyes, relieved that she wouldn't have to disappoint Riley by telling her Jesse wasn't coming over tomorrow.

It was clear that her daughter was totally besotted with Jesse, and the thought of Riley getting hurt had nearly sent her into a panic.

She'd tried so hard to protect her daughter from life's hurts that it was simply second nature to her now. She reacted to any real or perceived threat to her child, to any situation that could cause her harm.

As she thought about the day, and Jesse, Hannah realized that as much as she wanted to make sure that Jesse did nothing to hurt Riley, she also wanted to make certain he didn't hurt Tommy or the Ryans, either.

With a sigh, Hannah pushed her hair back and went to run her bath. Too bad she hadn't quite figured out if she'd done enough to protect *herself* from getting hurt.

He was having trouble sleeping. But Jesse figured that was simply because of the strange bed and the strange environment. Not to mention all that had happened in the past twenty-four hours. He hadn't had a minute to try to sort things out until now. And even now, he wasn't certain he could untangle the web of confusion and memories.

Lying in bed, staring at the ceiling, Jesse turned and surveyed the room. It was a child's room, he realized. *His* old room.

Painted in a deep shade of blue, the walls were decorated with wallpaper that boasted gaily colored ships and boats. The windows had matching curtains tied back with a thick white rope resembling a sailor's knot, allowing a hint of the moon or sun in.

The bed itself was small, a twin, he guessed, considering the fact that at six-four, his feet were now hanging off the end like a pair of wayward snowshoes. The spread was a deep blue as well, and atop the bed, he'd found a small plastic sailboat and a stuffed animal, a one-eared dog with sad, droopy eyes, or rather an eye, and a paw that had obviously been split and mended many times.

In one corner was a bookcase, spilling over with picture books and more plastic models of boats. Schooners, sailboats, even a tanker. A bureau sat against another wall, its top covered with aged photographs. In a corner, a lone basketball sat forgotten and forlorn. Nestled in the small bright blue beanbag chair in another corner was a weathered baseball, clearly well used. It was, he'd decided with a smile, a typical little boy's room.

When he'd first walked into the room, he'd merely stood in the doorway, staring, hoping to feel or remember something.

It hadn't happened and he was surprised by the pang of disappointment he'd felt.

Tommy had told him nothing had been changed in his room since the day he'd disappeared. Concerned that Jesse might be uncomfortable, Tommy had offered to put him in one of the rooms in the guest wing, but Jesse had refused, hoping that perhaps being back in his old bedroom might bring back some memories.

Antsy, Jesse got up from the bed and walked to the

bureau. Squinting, he bent down to study the framed photographs. There was one of a little boy and Tommy, both laughing. Jesse picked it up.

Tommy was standing on the front lawn of this very house. The little boy he was holding was clearly delighted that his grandfather was playing with him. Dressed in what looked like too-big bathing trunks, at the moment the boy was hanging upside down, his arms swinging free, nearly touching the ground. There was a wide toothless grin on his youthful face.

Sinking down on the bed, Jesse continued to stare at the photo. It had been summer, blisteringly hot that day, he suddenly remembered, and he and his brothers had been out back swimming in the pool. Unlike his brothers, he wasn't allowed in the pool alone, so when his brothers got tired of swimming, he knew he'd have to get out of the pool, too. Instead, he ran around the front of the house to find his grandfather, knowing Tommy would always come for a swim with him.

A soft knock on his bedroom door startled Jesse out of his memories and he glanced up.

''Come in,'' he called quietly. It was well past midnight. He thought everyone had turned in for the night.

The door slowly creaked open and Jared poked his head in. ''Jesse, you still awake?''

''Yeah,'' he said with a smile, glancing down at the picture again.

''I saw the light on.'' Jared shifted nervously. ''I had to get up with one of the twins. I hope you don't mind.''

''Not at all. Come on in.''

''You know, Jesse,'' Jared began softly, coming into

the room and glancing around, "every night for twenty years on my way to bed I walked past your bedroom, hoping against hope it was all a nightmare and I'd find you sound asleep, your covers kicked off, your pillow on the floor. But every night I'd be disappointed. Your room would be dark and empty." Jared sighed. "But tonight, when I walked past your room, there was a light shining under the door." Running a hand through his already sleep-rumpled hair, Jared's eyes burned from the enormous emotions swelling within. "I was almost afraid to open the door tonight. Afraid I'd open it and realize this whole day had been a dream, and the nightmare was what was real." Shaking his head, Jared blew out a weary breath, then dropped a hand to Jesse's shoulder. "Jesse, I don't know how to say this, but…I'm sorry." Tears blurred Jared's vision for a moment as he looked at his brother.

"You're sorry?" Jesse scowled. "For what?"

"I was your older brother, Jesse, I should have protected you, taken care of you, looked out for you." Jared had to pause to keep his emotions under control. "It should never have happened. For every day of these twenty years I felt responsible for what happened."

"You shouldn't have," Jesse replied. "It wasn't your fault or your responsibility. What happened, happened." Jesse shrugged. "I reckon there's no sense feeling guilty about something you had no control over." Jesse hadn't expected this, he realized. Hadn't expected to feel this enormous emotional connection to the Ryan men. *His brothers,* he thought, still getting used to the idea.

"Yeah, well, try telling that to a kid who's lost his

little brother.'' Jared gave Jesse's shoulder a squeeze. ''I just want you to know how sorry I am that this happened to you, to us, to Tommy. And how happy I am that you're home again.''

''Thanks,'' Jesse said quietly, moved too much to speak. For the first time in a long time he hadn't inwardly flinched at the mention of the word *home.*

''And Jesse, I don't care what happens in the future, I want you to remember something. I'll always be your brother,'' Jared said firmly, setting his jaw in a way that all the Ryan men did. ''I don't know what your future plans are, but whatever they are, wherever they may take you, whatever you may do, I want you to know, no matter what, I'm always here for you. That's a promise.''

Jesse fingered the photograph in his hand, too touched to speak. He'd never known the luxury of having someone—a brother—in his corner to back him up no matter what. And he realized he liked the thought. Felt comfortable with it, something he never thought he would be.

Grace had been very reclusive, keeping to herself, teaching him to do the same. As a kid, he'd never really questioned it. He grew up a loner, keeping to himself, determined not to want or need anyone else.

Now he understood Grace's obsessive need for privacy and why they kept to themselves. She must have lived in fear of someone finding out that he wasn't her real son. Jesse sighed. She made it seem as if it was him and her against the world, and he wasn't old enough or smart enough to even question her behavior.

Until now.

He'd never really had any male figures in his life, he realized. Not a father. A brother. Nothing. Kind of like Riley, he thought wistfully, understanding her need for a male influence and her instant attachment to him.

There'd been foremen on the ranch when Jesse was growing up and he got along well enough with them, but there'd been no emotional connection between them, he realized suddenly. And perhaps that was the difference.

"Thanks, Jared," he said softly, glancing up at his brother and feeling that connection, that emotional connection that ran deep, as if it was an inherent part of him, flow gently through him like a welcome river. "I appreciate it." He had to clear his throat. "And I appreciate all the hospitality as well."

"Well, we intend to make you earn your keep," Jared said with a laugh. "I understand you've been running your own spread down in Texas."

"That's right, but it sure is nothing compared to this."

"Well, I can always use a hand if you've got a free one." Jared rubbed his stubbled jaw and stifled a yawn. "Josh is busy most days with his law practice in town. And Jake, well, ranching has never been his idea of a good time. He'd rather be out chasing down a new deal. He handles all new land and business acquisitions for the family." Jared shrugged. "But that's their thing. Mine is the land." Jared walked to the window and glanced out. "It's always been this way, I guess."

"You always loved it, Jared, even as a kid."

Jared turned abruptly. "You remember that?"

Jesse looked as startled as Jared. "Yeah," he said

slowly. "I reckon I do." He frowned, trying to catch the memory before it dissipated. "I remember we used to go lie down by the creek and talk about the day when we were old enough to run the place ourselves."

"That's right," Jared said quietly, surprised his brother remembered.

"And you were always good with the animals and the help."

"Still am," Jared admitted with a hint of pride. "But I still can't handle the building and repairs. Much as I try, I can't get ahead of it, and quite frankly it bores me to tears."

"Well, I'll be happy to help any way I can." While I'm here, Jesse thought of adding, then changed his mind.

Jared glanced down at the picture Jesse still had in his hand. "That was always your favorite picture," he said with a smile. "Every time Mom and Dad or Tommy had to go out of town on business, you'd sleep with that picture." Jared chuckled. "Of course, in the morning all your covers might be on the floor, along with your pillow, but that picture would be firmly tucked in your arms."

Jesse smiled. "Yeah, I was just sitting here looking at it." He glanced up at Jared. "I was remembering the day it was taken." He laughed suddenly. "Josh was at a friend's house, but you and Jake were in the pool with me."

"We were trying to drown each other, no doubt," Jared said with a laugh.

"Yeah. And me as well. Mom wouldn't let me go swimming by myself, so when you and Jake wanted to go play ball with Luke next door, I knew I'd have to get out of the pool.'' Jesse grinned. ''So I went running around the front of the house to find Tommy because I reckon I knew he'd always go swimming with me.''

''You remember all of that?'' Jared asked carefully.

''Yeah.'' Jesse blew out a breath, then glanced up at his brother. ''Didn't reckon I remembered anything until I picked up this picture.'' He shook his head. ''It's funny, until I drove past Hannah's house I didn't rightly remember anything at all. My life seemed to begin in Texas. But since I've been here, certain things will trigger a memory so clear it's as if it just happened today. And then again, other things, things I try to remember, I just can't seem to. It's a mite frustrating, I tell you, Jared. Truly.''

Jared squeezed Jesse's shoulder again, then smiled down at him, wishing he could relieve his worry. ''Don't worry about it, Jesse. Just give yourself some time.'' Jared smiled. ''Time takes care of everything.''

Jesse glanced up suddenly, his eyes cloudy and confused. ''Jared?'' His eyebrows drew together in a frown of concentration that had Jared coming to attention.

''Yeah, Jesse?''

''Didn't our mother use to say that all the time?'' He could hear her voice, soft and lilting, as if it was coming down from a long, dark tunnel. Jesse's eyes slid closed.

*''Jesse, honey, don't you worry. You'll be as old as your brothers one day. Time takes care of everything, honey. In time, you'll be twelve just like Jake. I prom-*

*ise. Now go out and play with your brothers and stop fretting on such a beautiful day.''*

*Mama.*

He could see her standing in the kitchen, leaning against the counter, listening patiently to him. She was small and delicate, not much bigger than Hannah, he supposed. Dressed in a pair of slim jeans and a sweat-shirt that swamped her, she had flour all over her. On her jeans, her sweatshirt, on her feet, which were bare, and she smelled of something sweet and familiar.

Jesse laughed suddenly and his eyes flew open and he felt that unmistakable shiver of recognition roll over him. It had happened enough times now that it was becoming commonly familiar.

''Yeah,'' Jared admitted with a smile, doing a little remembering of his own. ''She used to say that all the time to us.'' He laughed. ''Almost every time one of us started complaining about something.''

''Yeah,'' Jesse said quietly. ''I remember.'' He frowned again. ''Jared, did she do a lot of baking or something? Something she'd use flour for?''

Jared laughed. ''She was famous for her apple pies. Every Friday, Mom would be up and in the kitchen bright and early, preparing the ingredients for her special apple pies.''

Jesse laughed suddenly. ''And she used to get flour all over everything. The counters, the floors, the table, and especially herself.''

''That's right.'' Jared smiled at the pleasant memory. ''Dad always used to say if she wasn't careful someone might pop *her* in the oven one day.''

"Vanilla," Jesse said abruptly, glancing up at Jared. "That's why she always smelled like vanilla."

Jared shrugged, not certain of the importance. "I guess so, Jesse."

"Vanilla," Jesse said again with a shake of his head. "I didn't remember that until this moment." If he tried hard enough, he could almost smell her. He shook his head suddenly, another piece of the puzzle sliding into place. "Now I know why I can't handle the smell of vanilla." He looked at Jared. "It makes me ill and I never knew why." Jesse glanced down at the picture he still held in his hand, his fingers tightening. "It's because it reminded me of our mother." His words hung in the air for a long, silent moment.

Jared shifted uncomfortably. "She loved you very much, Jesse. You were her youngest son. She never got over losing you."

Unable to speak, Jesse simply nodded, feeling an overwhelming sense of loss he simply couldn't explain. It was like a raw, open wound of grief in his heart, leeching through every inch of his being.

"Well, look, it's late, I'd better get back to bed or I won't get any sleep before it's time to get up for the next feeding." Jared hesitated a moment, his hand still on Jesse's shoulder. "Thanks, Jesse."

"For what?"

Jared's smile was slow. "For coming home, bro. For coming home."

*Home.*

Jesse sighed. Maybe, just maybe for the first time in his life, he was beginning to understand exactly what the word *home* meant. But it was a struggle, he had to admit. A real struggle, and he was torn by so many conflicting emotions of where home was, and more importantly, where he belonged.

His eyes slid closed and memories of his mother, his *real* mother, flashed through his mind. So fast he wanted to slow them down, savor them like a long-lost beloved book recently found.

The grief he felt when he thought of his mother—of his own loss—was too profound for him to contain the emotions the recovered memory of her evoked.

He'd lost her in so many ways, he thought. Lost her, and worse, lost all of his memories of her. And that, he realized, was the real tragedy.

How could he not have remembered her? he wondered, feeling a profound sense of shame mixed with grief. How could he have simply erased any memory of someone he'd loved so deeply, instinctively, the way only a child could love his mother?

Jesse shook his head.

He didn't know.

With a sigh, he lay across the bed, then tried again to recall, to remember who Jesse Ryan had been. The desire to know was suddenly immediate and urgent, as if it was the most important thing in the world. And maybe at the moment it was, he thought.

If he remembered who Jesse Ryan had been, perhaps then he'd know who *he* really was.

And then finally he'd be able to go...*home.*

Hannah glanced up at the Ferris wheel in absolute horror. "Oh no, Jesse. No." Raising her hands in the air, she took a self-protective step back and furiously shook her head.

The Saddle Falls carnival had arrived in town just for the weekend. It was an annual event held the weekend before the start of school again at the end of January. There were rides, arcades, fortune-tellers and food kiosks offering anything a person could want.

It was a traditional outing for the Ryan clan, and she and Riley had always been included. This year Jesse had invited both her and Riley, and they'd gone together as a threesome, meeting the rest of the family at Tonoto's pizza parlor for dinner before heading toward the carnival.

The Ryans always donated the parking lot of the Saddle Falls Hotel to the carnival operators to use, and the sheriff made sure Main Street and all the connecting side streets were closed to ensure public safety.

Electric carnival lights had been strung up around the perimeter of the enormous hotel parking lot and now lit up the entire area like a bright noonday.

The crowd was enormous, drawing from the entire town of Saddle Falls as well as all the smaller towns surrounding it.

Hannah glanced up at the Ferris wheel again and felt her stomach pitch and roll. She shook her head once more, ignoring the amusement in Jesse's eyes.

"Now, for the past week or so I've gone along with just about every harebrained idea you had about showing me how to have…fun." Hannah almost choked on the last word. "But I draw the line at climbing aboard something that's going to send me soaring into the sky." She scowled at him, trying not to be charmed by the look on his face. It was hard, she realized, when he was standing there holding her beloved daughter in his arms, and they were wearing identical, mischievous grins.

"Come on, Mama, it will be fun," Riley encouraged, reaching out an arm to wrap it around her mother's neck to draw her closer. Riley succeeded in drawing her mother close, but Hannah was also just that much closer to Jesse. And it made her nervous. "Uncle Jesse said so."

"Uncle Jesse said so," Hannah muttered under her breath. Uncle Jesse had been saying a lot of things the past week, she realized. To her. To Riley.

And she didn't know who was more enamored of him, Hannah thought with a weary sigh. Her. Or her daughter.

In either case, looking at the love and adoration shining in her daughter's eyes, Hannah realized that this could turn out to be quite a disastrous situation.

Riley had taken to Jesse in a way she'd never taken to another man before, not even Jake, Jared or Josh. The little girl had pretty much adopted Jesse as her own.

But she herself wasn't any better, Hannah realized dully. She'd been spending as much time being charmed by the blasted man as her daughter. It was just so odd. She normally didn't trust men. Not any of them. Not that she let men get close enough to her *to* trust. And for some reason, perhaps because of their shared history and past, she trusted Jesse. Instinctively and totally.

As a friend, she reminded herself, trying to keep her

feelings and emotions balanced and curb the fear over the feelings she couldn't deny.

But she was an adult, much better at understanding these kinds of life situations.

Unfortunately, Riley was just a child and didn't understand that just because Jesse was a part of their lives for now, it didn't mean he would be permanently. And the thought worried Hannah because she didn't want to see her daughter hurt when Jesse left, and he would leave, she realized. He'd made that clear in every way every day.

As much as Riley longed for and needed a strong male figure in her life, Hannah couldn't let her daughter become too dependent on Jesse.

She knew it, but at the moment she wasn't certain how to prevent it. Hannah glanced at her daughter again and felt a swell of loving protectiveness. If it wasn't too late already, Hannah thought with a sigh, shoving her hair back from her forehead to glance up at the dreaded carnival ride again.

"Mama, please?" Riley begged, her lower lip sliding into a pout. "I really wanna go. Pul-lease?" Riley was doing her best imitation of a poor neglected child deprived of her heart's desire.

"Riley, honey—"

"Now, darlin', you're not afraid, are you?" Jesse teased, sliding his free arm around Hannah's waist and drawing her even closer. A hint of his scent, so achingly familiar now, teased her nostrils and caused her toes to tighten in her shoes.

"Afraid?" she repeated, trying to sound brave and failing miserably. "Absolutely not," she insisted with a stubborn lift of her chin. "It's just...just...if I'd been meant to go flying around the sky, I'm sure I would have been born with an engine, wings and a couple of propellers."

Hannah had always prided herself on never showing any weakness in front of her daughter. Never showing any fear, especially not of heights. She was Riley's total security and stability; it wouldn't do for her daughter to feel she couldn't handle something.

"You're funny, Mama," Riley said with a giggle. "But can I go, even if you don't want to?" She beamed at Jesse, winding her arm tighter around his neck. "I won't be afraid if Uncle Jesse's there, Mama. Honest."

Torn, Hannah glanced from her daughter to Jesse, not certain if she was amused or annoyed by Riley's unfailing belief in Jesse. Something else for her to worry about.

She was just doing this—spending so much time with Jesse—to protect Tommy and the Ryans, she assured herself. At least if she was around Jesse and the family, she could keep an eye on him and make sure nothing went wrong.

In addition, Jesse seemed to be far more comfortable when she was there and his family was around. Almost as if she was a conduit, bridging the gap between them. A role she happily would play if it meant ensuring Tommy's happiness.

But she had to be realistic. As much time as she was spending with Jesse was also time Riley was spending with him, and getting more and more attached to him day by day.

As was Hannah. And she knew better than to get emotionally involved with a man who wasn't permanent. Or more importantly with a man who couldn't see the value of family, especially his own. Like Jesse. Like Riley's father, she thought. She'd already lived through that once, and would never make that mistake again. Not just for her sake, but her Riley's as well.

No, she realized, blowing out a breath and glaring at the carnival ride, she had to keep her feelings in perspective in order to protect her daughter. That was her first priority.

She'd just have to monitor the situation with Riley carefully, she reasoned.

"Come on, darlin'," Jesse said, leaning down to whisper in Hannah's ear as his fingers tightened around her waist, drawing her even closer to tenderly brush his lips against her temple, sending a chill racing through her. The temptation to lean into him, against him, to quiet some of the longings that had been building each day since the moment she'd laid eyes on him was strong. But she resisted them. Barely.

"It'll be fun," Jesse promised. "And I promise to keep you safe." He laughed when she gave him a wild look. "Hey, you're gonna bruise my masculinity, here." Eyes twinkling, Jesse grinned. "Most women would feel safe with a big guy like me."

She laughed. "I'm sure, Jesse, but I'm not most women." The moment the words were out, she regretted them, realizing how they sounded. She wasn't angry or bitter, simply realistic. Most women had been able to trust and lean on a man at some time in their life. Either a father, a boyfriend, a husband. Her father had never been around long enough to lean on, and when he was around, he was too busy with his far flung business interests and his concern with impressing his friends to pay any attention to his daughters. And the only boyfriend, if you could call him that, she'd ever had was Riley's father, and she certainly couldn't trust or depend on him for anything.

"Darlin', I reckon that's a real shame, then," Jesse said quietly, realizing that his gut feeling that someone had hurt her deeply was probably right on target. Every protective instinct inside him, the instinct to protect one of your own, surged to the fore, surprising him.

The idea of someone hurting Hannah made his fists curl. Worse, the idea that she felt as if she had never been able to trust a man made him feel sad for her.

Although he wanted to know everything about her past, he decided now wasn't the time to pry. Not with Riley sitting within earshot. He was a patient man. He could wait. But he made a note to ask Hannah about it the next time they were alone.

"Well, darlin', I guess you're gonna have to learn that there are some men in this world you can trust." His gaze, somber, steady and oh-so-reassuring, met hers. "Remember what I told you that first day in your backyard?" he asked quietly.

"I remember," she admitted dismally, realizing just how her response had sounded. "That you don't make promises you can't keep."

"That's right, darlin'." Cocking his head, he looked at her. "Don't you believe me?" he asked at the look on her face.

"No. I mean I believe you, Jesse, but...but—"

"But what?"

"If I get sick, Jesse Ryan, I swear I'm going to strangle you," she muttered as he laughed.

"Come on, darlin'." He pressed a kiss to her temple. "I promise you'll be safe and it'll be fun." He drew back and looked at her for a long moment. "I would never let anything happen to you, Hannah-Anna," he whispered. "You're safe as long as you're with me." He ran a finger down her nose then grinned. "And that, darlin', is a promise."

Too stunned to respond, Hannah let him take her hand to lead her to the line waiting for a ride on the Ferris wheel.

"I always wanted to kiss a pretty girl while sitting atop one of these things," Jesse admitted as the attendant carefully strapped the three of them into the first empty swinging seat.

"Uncle Jesse, you can kiss me," Riley offered, nearly bouncing in her seat in excitement and lifting her face for his kiss. He laughed and obliged by planting a loud kiss on her cheek.

"Can I kiss you again when we get to the top?" he asked, nuzzling his nose against hers.

"Yep." Riley grinned, craning her neck to see as much as possible, wiggling in her seat and making the entire thing sway back and forth. Hannah gritted her teeth tightly together, praying her stomach would stop swaying and dipping, fearing everything in it was about to reappear.

Eyes wide with adoration, Riley grinned. "You can kiss me anytime, Uncle Jesse."

Jesse draped an arm around Riley as well as Hannah,

drawing both of them close until they were pressed against them. ''Well, darlin', I do believe I'll take you up on your offer.'' He was looking at Hannah when he said it. His mouth was inviting and more than tempting. If she closed her eyes she could actually remember the feel of his lips against hers. The taste of him. The strength of his arms as he wrapped them around her, pulling her close to the hardness of that incredible body.

Hannah wanted to groan in frustration. She was flushed, warm, and if this ride didn't get going pretty soon, she was going to jump out of her skin in anticipation, not certain if it was from the fear of the ride or the fear of knowing Jesse was going to kiss her again.

It meant nothing, she assured herself, turning to stare out over the parking lot. In the past week, Jesse had kissed her numerous times, but as a friend, she told herself. Nothing more. He'd kissed Rebecca, Emma, and Natalie, she thought.

But not quite the same way he'd kissed her, she had to admit.

But she wasn't about to read anything into it. Jesse was just being...friendly. That's all, she reasoned. No use borrowing something to worry about when she had plenty of real things to worry about.

With a jerk that almost had her fighting for freedom, the ride started and Hannah gripped the handlebar tightly, trying not to let the fear inside her show.

''Relax, darlin', I promise you're safe,'' Jesse whispered, turning to her, hating the fear he saw in her eyes and realizing how little trust she had. For him. For everyone. And he couldn't help but wonder what on earth, or who on earth, had put that fear into her.

"Easy for you to say," she muttered, clinging tighter to the bar and leaning into him. He was strong and steady, and he wasn't...moving. At the moment it was something to be grateful for.

"Look, Mama, I could almost see our house." Riley pointed, her arm extending out of the swinging seat, and Hannah's heart plunged.

"Riley, please, keep your hands inside."

"Careful, darlin'," Jesse whispered in Hannah's ear. "You're going to frighten her. If she senses your fear, you'll transmit it to her, and then she'll be afraid of heights as well."

"I...I...can't help it," Hannah admitted, giving him a woeful look as the ride slowly made its way around the cycle. She knew Jesse was right, but at the moment could do little about it. Struggling to look composed, Hannah scowled as the ground moved farther and farther away. "I hate heights."

"Good thing you're not any taller than you are then, darlin'," he teased. "Or you'd be in big trouble."

She laughed. She couldn't believe it was possible to laugh when her stomach was in knots, her heart was tumbling, her nerves thrumming and her knuckles so white they hurt.

As the ride slowed, then finally stopped at the top, her eyes were clenched shut.

"Look, Mama, I can see all the way forever."

She didn't want to look. She wanted to get down and have the solid, stable, *stationary* ground underneath her. And she wasn't ever leaving it again, she decided.

"Open your eyes, darlin'," Jesse coaxed, his arm warm around her, his breath soft and feathering over her ear again, making her shiver. "It's quite a spectacular sight."

Clenching her teeth tightly together, Hannah forced herself to slowly open her eyes. Her breath caught. "It's...beautiful," she admitted, staring across the entire expanse of the town. The stark contrast of the stars sparkling like diamonds on fire against a black backdrop of sky was magical. The moon was high, a small sickle of white with shadows radiating off it as if it were a living, breathing thing. The entire town of Saddle Falls was spread out below, dazzling in display, making her heart ache with love for her home. "Just beautiful," she said again, swallowing a lump.

"So are you," Jesse whispered against her ear, nearly making her bolt out of the seat again. "So are you." He pressed closer until his lips were trailing across her ear. "Can I have my kiss now that we're at the top?" He drew back to gaze at her, grinning at the look of fear and bewilderment in her eyes. If he didn't know better, he'd think she hadn't been kissed before.

"Do I have to go on this thing again?" she asked suspiciously, not too proud to barter for a safer perch if necessary.

"Guess that depends on the kiss," he teased, leaning forward to brush his lips seductively over hers. Slowly, back and forth until the heat built and Hannah wasn't certain if her stomach was dipping from his kiss or from the ride.

"Jesse." She drew back and laid a hand to his chest, more shaken than she could remember.

"My turn, Uncle Jesse," Riley said.

"No, darlin'," he said, turning to her with a smile. "It's my turn." He pointed a finger to his cheek. "Right here will be fine." Riley leaned over and planted a loud kiss on his cheek, then blew it into a raspberry, making herself and Jesse giggle.

"Your turn, Mama."

"What?" Hannah blinked at her daughter.

"It's your turn to kiss Uncle Jesse," Riley said, reaching out to grab the handlebar. She wiggled it and the car tipped forward a bit, nearly making Hannah screech.

"Riley, please," Hannah said, pressing a hand to her tummy. "I'll...I'll kiss Uncle Jesse if you promise to sit still." Hannah took a deep breath. "Perfectly still."

Riley shrugged. "'Kay, Mama."

Hannah fully intended to kiss his cheek, just as her daughter had, but at the last minute Jesse turned his head and her mouth caught his, just in the corner. It was like tasting only a tiny bit of forbidden fruit, making her long for a full, satisfying bite. Hannah did her best not to groan as Jesse's arm tightened around her, bringing her close until her nipples hardened in response as he deepened the kiss. She could feel the soft, gentle touch of his tongue brushing against her lips, sending a hot, wicked thrill coursing through her.

Leaning into him, she clutched the front of his shirt, simply out of fear, she told herself, holding on to him in an effort to keep him close. When the ride jerked again as it started its descent downward—and backward—Hannah pulled back, breathless and stunned, to grip the handlebar for dear life.

"Uncle Jesse, do you like our town?" Riley asked.

Drawing both females closer to him, Jesse rested his head against Riley's, as content as he could remember. "Well, darlin', I reckon I do."

"Lots?"

He laughed. Everything to this child was a degree of one extreme or the other. It totally amused him.

"Yes, darlin', lots." He glanced down at Hannah. "And I'm beginning to like it more and more."

Delighted, Hannah lifted her head. "Does that mean—"

He cut her off with a quick kiss. "All that means is that I'm surely enjoying my time here." He kissed her again, noting the disappointment in her eyes. "I'm here now, Hannah," he said quietly. "Let's just enjoy this moment, okay?"

Hannah simply stared at him for a moment, wondering how she was ever going to change his mind, get him to accept the Ryans as family and Saddle Falls as his home.

She didn't know, but she realized she'd better figure out something, because she had a feeling time was running out.

## *Chapter Six*

"Would you like something to drink, Jesse?" Hannah asked, sinking onto the front step of her porch next to him. They'd walked home from the carnival with Jesse carrying a sleeping Riley in his arms.

It was a wonderful feeling to have friends and neighbors, people she'd known her whole life—people who'd also known Jesse as a boy, and knew what had happened to him—stop and say hello or wave. It was one of the things she'd always loved about living in a small town.

"No, thanks. I had enough food and drink at the carnival to last me a week." He chuckled, then patted his flat stomach. "I can't imagine where Riley puts everything," he said with a shake of his head, turning to look at Hannah. In the quiet darkness of the night, the nearest streetlight was at least a quarter of a mile away, so it was as if they were cocooned in their own private world. Other than the stars above and the soft yellow porch light, it was dark and quiet.

Hannah was sitting directly under the soft yellow light and it shadowed the planes and angles of her face, drifting over her mouth, highlighting how beautiful she was.

"I'd swear she has a hollow leg, as my mama would have said," Jesse observed.

Hannah's face sobered for a moment at the mention of his mother. "You mean Grace Garland?" she asked carefully, and he shook his head.

"No, darlin'," he said with a smile, touching her hand. "I meant my mother. My *real* mother," he said softly.

"Jesse, you remembered her?" Hannah asked in some surprise.

He blew out a breath and turned to look at the dark, quiet street. "Yeah. One night Jared and I were talking. It was late, after everyone had gone to bed." He smiled, remembering their conversation as he turned to her again. "I'd been looking at some pictures in my room, pictures from when I was a kid." He shook his head. "It brought back some memories I'd never realized I had until then."

"That's wonderful, Jesse," she said, more than pleased. Day by day he seemed to be remembering more and more. Hopefully, in time, he'd be able to remember everything, including the fact that Saddle Falls was his home. And the Ryans were and always would be his family.

"Yeah, darlin', I reckon it is." He lifted her hand,

brought it to his lips for a gentle kiss, then held on to it, linking his fingers through hers. He had strong, fine hands. Large and masculine with a rough hint of calluses. Working-man's hands, she thought.

"Jesse?"

"Yeah, darlin'?"

With a yawn of contentment, Hannah stretched out her legs. "Riley had a wonderful time tonight." She gave his hand a squeeze, aware of the way her pulse was scrambling. "Thank you."

"For what?" he asked in surprised, skimming a finger across her chin to tuck a stray strand of hair behind her ear.

Hannah glanced away, suddenly feeling self-conscious. "For being so wonderful with her. To her."

"Darlin', she's an incredible little girl." He chuckled. "I can't imagine anyone not being wonderful to her." He studied Hannah's face, aware of the pulsing need of desire that had been simmering between them the past week.

"You know, you're going to make a wonderful father," she said quietly, almost immediately regretting the comment the moment it was out, not wanting him to misinterpret it.

"Well, I reckon it's no secret I love kids," he said with a smile.

She cocked her head to look at him. The amber glow from the light glanced off his face, shadowing it in softness. "Jesse, how come you're not married?" She'd been thinking about it, wondering about it, and just had never found the time to ask him.

He shrugged. "Guess I never found the right

woman.'' His gaze was steady on hers, and for a moment she wondered if he'd deliberately tightened his hand on hers. The look on his face made her heart flip over. ''And if the truth be told, I reckon I haven't had much time to look. It was always just me and Ma, and she wasn't one for too much socializing. I've always been a loner, I guess, not comfortable around a lot of people, and we kept mostly to ourselves. Growing up, it never occurred to me that might be odd. Now, of course, I understand the reason for it, but at the time it just seemed normal. Then the older I got, the more responsibility I took on at the ranch until I was running it full-time, especially the past few years since college.'' Jesse shrugged. ''And you know how time-consuming running a ranch is. Then Ma got sick, and well...'' His voice trailed off and he glanced at Hannah sheepishly, wondering how she'd react to him calling Grace his mother. Especially after just referring to Janice Ryan as his mother. Dragging his free hand through his hair, Jesse realized his emotions were still a tangled mess. ''I guess because I'd always been such a loner, growing up and all, it was real hard for me to let people—''

''You mean women,'' she interjected with a smile. He nodded, then grinned.

''Yeah, women close to me.'' He shrugged again. ''I was engaged once,'' he admitted. ''But I realized that I just couldn't seem to unlock my emotions and let them go, not even with her. I knew then I couldn't marry her, it wouldn't be fair or right.''

''What happened?'' Hannah asked quietly, aching for Jesse and wondering how much of his blocked and locked emotions had to do with what had happened to him when he was five.

"I told her the truth." His smile was wan. "She was not a happy camper, I'll tell you that, but in the end I guess she realized it was for the best as well. She knew I was emotionally closed, or as she called it, 'emotionally vacant,' and for the life of me I couldn't convince her it wasn't her. It was me." He turned to Hannah, a look of confusion on his face. "I don't know why, Hannah. Truly. It's just something inside me that locks up my emotions and I just can't let them go, can't seem to let people get close to me, nor can I let myself go and just...feel something deep for someone."

"Jesse," she began carefully, her heart aching for him. "Did you ever consider that maybe that was a result of what happened to you? The trauma of being torn from your family, your home and everything that was familiar when you were such a young boy?"

"It occurred to me," he admitted. "The last few months at least. But you've got to remember, for most of my life I wasn't even aware that I'd been kidnapped. Or that Grace Garland wasn't my mother, my family. Or that I was someone else. So how would I be able to equate the two?"

"You're right," Hannah said with an understanding smile. No wonder he'd never been able to examine what might have been the cause for his emotional cautiousness. "So you never got involved with anyone else?"

He chuckled. "Now, I didn't say that. I'm not a saint, Hannah, I like women as well as the next guy, but from that point on I made sure I didn't let anyone think that I was ready to make any kind of emotional commitment. I told you, I don't make promises I can't keep.'' He shrugged. ''I just figured it was something inside me that wouldn't allow me to let people close.''

''Now you know differently?'' she asked quietly.

''I'm not sure,'' he admitted honestly, knowing he'd let her and Riley closer than he'd ever let any woman—women—before. But for some reason it seemed perfectly natural, even normal. Certainly not something he was concerned about. Perhaps it was because Hannah was such an important part of his past, he reasoned. And she was familiar and comfortable.

''Since all this happened, Grace's death, finding out about Tommy and the Ryans and everything else has been an emotional upheaval unlike anything I've ever known. So I can't rightly say that it's changed anything inside me because I honestly don't know yet.'' He smiled. ''It hasn't been put to the test so to speak.'' He may recognize that he'd let Hannah and Riley close to him, but admitting it to her was not something he was comfortable with yet. It wasn't anything he'd ever experienced before. And until he understood it himself, he wasn't about to admit it.

On some deep level it frightened him as nothing else had. He had promised himself he'd remain detached while he was here in Saddle Falls. Detached and unemotional. He didn't plan on being here long and there was no point in getting involved with people who weren't going to be a part of his life.

So he wasn't quite ready to examine his feelings or the emotional attachment that had grown for Hannah and Riley. If he ignored it, then he didn't have to try to understand it. And right now when he was trying to understand so many things, he wasn't certain he could handle another.

Hannah nodded, wondering why his words made her so sad. He basically had just admitted that he couldn't get emotionally involved or attached to anyone. And that did not bode well for Tommy or the Ryans, she realized.

Or for her and Riley, her mind whispered.

"Now what about you, darlin'?" He released her hand and draped an arm around her shoulder, drawing her close so she was leaning against him. "How come you never married?"

Still thinking about his emotional temperature, she glanced up at him sharply. "How do you know I was never married?" she asked with a decided scowl.

"Tommy," he said simply, then grinned. "I've done my fair share of asking questions, Hannah." He lifted a hand in the air in a defensive gesture at the look on her face. "Hey, I'm trying to piece together my past and I can't do that without asking questions."

She understood that, but wasn't certain she liked the idea of him asking questions about *her* past.

"So, will you tell me about Riley's father?" He had to admit he had wondered about the man. Wondered how the man could walk away from his own child or let Hannah raise Riley alone.

In the week since he'd been here, he'd seen no evidence of a male presence in Riley's life. Or Hannah's, for that matter. Nor any evidence of family.

She turned to look at him, stunned by the question. "Why?" She rarely looked back. There was no point in regrets or recriminations. She tried to look only at the positive side. She had Riley, and that was all that mattered.

''Because I'd like to know.'' Gently, he laid a hand to her cheek. ''It's important to me, Hannah. Truly.'' He hesitated. ''I want to know who put that fear in your eyes. I want to know who made you feel as if you weren't safe with a man.''

Perhaps it was the way he said it or the way he looked at her that made the locks she kept around the memories come tumbling open and she found that she wanted to tell him, to confide in him.

It had been so long since she'd had another adult to talk to, to confide in, to pour out her heart to, especially a man her own age. She had Tommy of course, but she couldn't and wouldn't tell him of the pain she carried in her heart because of her parents.

No, she realized immediately, laying her head down on the soft curve of his shoulder and taking a deep breath. She'd *never* had a man as a confidant. Except for Jesse when they were children. With that reassuring thought, Hannah took a deep breath and decided to start slowly.

''Riley's father...well, I guess I'd better start at the beginning.'' She had to take another deep breath for courage and plunged in. ''You said you don't remember much about my parents.''

''Right, I don't.''

''Well, like Tommy, they settled in Saddle Falls when the town was still young. They made quite a fortune for themselves early on, even before my sister or I were born. My parents, unlike Tommy, weren't in the least bit interested in family.'' She hadn't realized how bitter her voice had become or how painful the memory still was even after all these years. ''They didn't have time for either me or my sister. I rarely saw them, Jesse, and I certainly didn't have any kind of home life like all of you Ryans. Me and my sister were left with nannies or nurses while my parents went gallivanting all around the world, enjoying their fortune and impressing their friends.''

''And ignoring their children?'' Jesse interjected quietly, feeling his guts twist in discomfort at the thought of Hannah being a young girl left alone with strangers. No wonder she had such wariness and fear in her eyes. No wonder she felt so strongly about family.

''That's about it,'' Hannah admitted, forcing a smile though her lips were trembling. ''That's why I was always at your house. I loved anything to do with family. And I was so jealous and envious of the home and family life you had, Jesse.'' She had to swallow the lump in her throat for the shame she always felt for her jealousy. ''My father had had a few business dealings early on with Tommy, and he'd asked Tommy to be my godfather.'' She grinned. ''He agreed, which was probably the best thing that ever happened to me.'' This time her smile was real and genuine when she lifted her head to look at him, her gaze steady on his. ''Tommy was—is—the most wonderful, loving man I've ever met. Totally devoted to his family. And more importantly, he always considered me part of the family and included me in everything. My sister as well, but she wasn't very interested in family, at least not the way I was.'' Hannah shook her head. ''I don't know what I would have done without him. He was the only security I had through my entire childhood.''

Feeling his heart ache for the loneliness she must have felt as a child, Jesse kissed the top of her head. ''I'm sorry, darlin'.''

Absently, she blinked away a tear. ''That's why you and I were so close as kids, Jesse. I was always at your house. My sister never wanted me tagging around with her. We weren't close.'' She shrugged. ''We were the same age, and even though you had your brothers, because they were older than you, they often did things that you couldn't.''

''Like having a sleepover at Luke's,'' he said quietly, remembering the night he'd been kidnapped.

''Yeah,'' she replied softly. ''So while you were close to your brothers, you and I were also close.''

He nodded, understanding now why, from the moment he'd arrived in Saddle Falls and driven down Hannah's street and seen her house, there was something special about it and her.

''I wanted a family of my own so bad, Jesse. I didn't care about material things or wealth. I never wanted to be like my parents. People were important to me, not things.'' She had to take a breath, then brushed a wayward strand of hair from her face from a quick kick of breeze that whispered through the darkness. ''Anyway, when I was eighteen and right out of high school, my parents were staying in a villa in Europe for the summer. As a graduation present, they sent me a telegram and invited me for the summer.''

"Didn't they come to your graduation?" he asked in quiet surprise.

She shook her head. "No, Jesse. The only people at my graduation were the Ryans." She smiled in remembrance. "Tommy had a huge party for me. It was wonderful," she admitted. "And to tell you the truth, by that time I'd long given up hope of my parents ever changing, so it wasn't that big of a surprise."

Now he understood why she was so loyal and loving toward Tommy and all the Ryans. They were the family she'd never had but always wanted. "So did you go to Europe for the summer?"

She nodded. "My sister, who is five years older, had moved to Europe right after she graduated. She was engaged to some wealthy European and had quickly fit into my parents' lifestyle."

"But you didn't?"

Hannah laughed, but the sound was bitter. "I hated it," she admitted. "I love Saddle Falls, love the fact that I know everyone and everyone knows me. I hate parties and all that fancy socializing. It's just not me. I'm a small-town girl with small-town values. Home. Hearth. Family. That's all that's every mattered to me. Maybe because I never had it." She hesitated. "Anyway, during that summer I met a man who had been a business acquaintance of my father's. I thought he understood that I was not anything like my parents, that I wanted a different kind of life, and more than anything else a family." Her voice had grown cool and distant. "I thought he wanted the same things."

"Did he tell you that?" Jesse asked quietly, trying to understand.

"Yes," she admitted. "And I was young and wildly in love for the first time in my life. It never occurred to me that he would deceive me or lie to me."

"But he did?" Jesse asked, appalled that someone could be deliberately deceitful or cruel to Hannah.

She didn't answer but continued. "When I found out I was pregnant with Riley, I was so thrilled, Jesse." Hannah's voice went soft and wistful at the memory. "It was the happiest day of my life. I thought I was finally going to have the kind of family and family life I'd always wanted. I couldn't wait to tell Riley's father." Her voice changed so abruptly, he frowned.

"What happened, darlin'?" Jesse asked softly, feeling her entire body tense against him. Instinctively, he pulled her closer.

"He neglected to mention the fact that he was already married."

"What!" Jesse's eyebrows drew together and his free hand fisted in anger and frustration.

"He was already married and already had a family." She tried to smile but found she couldn't. The shame of being so naive, and contributing to the pain of another woman and family had never really left her. It was something she'd had to learn to live with. "And he sure didn't want another family since he wasn't particularly loving or faithful to the family he already had."

"Oh, darlin'." Jesse gathered her stiff body close to him, giving in to the urge to comfort, to care, gently sliding his hands up and down her back, feeling the warmth of her body heat beneath the thin cotton shirt she wore. The need that pulsed seemed to increase in tempo, becoming less lazy, a bit more urgent.

With a sniffle, Hannah cursed her emotions and vowed to get through the rest of her past without feeling sorry for herself.

It had taken her a long time to forgive herself, but now she finally had. Forgiven herself for wanting, yearning, longing for something she'd wanted for so very long, she allowed her emotions to overrule her common sense.

She imagined she wasn't the first woman to be fooled by a man she loved—and she probably wasn't the last.

With another sniffle, she went on. "Anyway, when I told him I was expecting, he was horrified. He wanted me to get rid of Riley. He didn't want my parents to know we'd been involved. He didn't want another child nor did he plan on divorcing his wife, who it turned out was the one who had the money that financed his lifestyle."

"But you didn't," Jesse said in admiration, trying to hide the intensity of feelings her words had aroused. He would be very happy for about ten minutes alone with the guy who'd done this to Hannah. And to Riley. Ten minutes would be more than enough to teach the man a thing or two about taking advantage of, using, and then discarding women.

"Absolutely not." With a fierceness that no longer surprised him, Hannah shook her head. "I wasn't about to destroy my own child, a child I desperately wanted and loved from the moment she was conceived."

He chuckled. "And you think you had to tell me

that?'' he asked with a smile and a shake of his head. ''All anyone has to do is look at you when Riley's around and they can see the pride and joy on your face.''

Hannah grinned, unashamed of the love and pride she'd always had in her precious daughter. ''She is my pride and my joy, Jesse. She always has been.''

''As she should be.'' Jesse was thoughtful for a moment. ''Hannah, why didn't your parents do something?''

''They did,'' she admitted with a wan smile. ''They disowned me.''

''Excuse me?'' Scowling, Jesse was certain he'd heard her wrong. ''What do you mean they disowned you?'' he asked, trying to make sense of this.

Hannah shrugged. ''When I told my parents I was expecting, they were appalled. Their youngest daughter was nineteen, unwed and about to become a mother. It certainly didn't fit in with the plans they'd had. I had become an embarrassing problem to them. I honestly don't think they were as worried about me as they were about what their high-society friends would say.'' Hannah shrugged, remembering the pain and fear she had experienced at the time, knowing she was all alone and on her own and about to become a mother. Her unmitigated joy had almost overshadowed her fear. Almost. ''My parents told me to either get rid of the child, marry the father or they'd disown me.'' She moved her shoulders restlessly. ''My father was apparently involved in some high-profile international merger at the time with a lot of very socially prominent people and it was clear they wanted to present a picture-perfect family.'' She gave a brittle laugh. ''It's funny. Not once did they ask me if I wanted the baby. Or if I loved or wanted to marry the father.'' She pushed her hair off her face. ''That apparently was secondary to their needs.''

Tension coiled through him and Jesse's eyebrows drew together. ''And did you happen to mention to them that this creep was already married?''

''No.'' She hesitated a moment, wondering if he'd be able to understand. ''I was far too proud to tell my parents what a fool I'd been because I knew that they'd just find fault with me and insist that I get rid of my baby. Getting pregnant while unmarried was one thing, getting pregnant by a man already married, well...'' Her voice trailed off and instinctively she placed a hand on her stomach, remembering the joy she felt when Riley was growing within her.

''So you never told them the truth about Riley's father?'' he asked quietly, aching for the pain and fear she must have had at a time when she'd probably desperately needed love and support.

She shook her head. ''There was no point. I wasn't going to marry him and I wasn't going to get rid of my baby.'' She shrugged. ''So I came home and gave birth to Riley alone.''

''Your parents didn't relent? Didn't help you?'' Jesse couldn't prevent his own anger from seeping into his words. But he simply couldn't imagine parents abandoning their own daughter like that.

She laughed, but the sound was bitter. ''Not one whit,'' she said quietly. ''I shamed them and embarrassed them in front of their friends and I completely rejected their lifestyle. To say nothing of the fact that I refused to tell them who the father was. I wanted nothing more than to come back home to Saddle Falls and make a life here.'' With a smile of pleasure and contentment she glanced around in the darkness. She knew every tree, every sound, every home in town. There was a comfort and security about Saddle Falls that never failed to soothe her. ''I had no intention of spending my life flitting to party after party while leaving my child alone to be raised by someone else.'' She studied his face, then shook her head, the sadness clearly etched in her face. ''And Jesse, to be honest, I was furious with them. I never understood how that beautiful little girl sleeping upstairs in her bedroom could be looked at as anybody's shame.''

''I agree, darlin','' Jesse said, realizing Hannah and Riley were probably better off without her family. ''She is a wonderful child, darlin', one anyone would be proud to claim as their own.''

''They never even saw Riley,'' Hannah continued softly. ''My parents were killed in a boating accident when Riley was just six months old. They left everything to my sister.'' Hannah glanced up at the old house she'd grown up in with affection. ''Except for this house. I don't know why, but they left this house in trust for Riley.'' Hannah shrugged. ''I don't know, maybe it was their way of making up for what they'd done.'' Hannah smiled. ''See, in their minds, even as a final act, they thought leaving their grandchild a thing, a possession, was important. It would have been a lot more important for Riley to have had her grandparents' love.''

"Darlin', from what I can tell, Riley hasn't suffered any. You've done a wonderful job with her. She's a loving, caring little girl, and you should be mighty proud of her. And of yourself," he added. "It couldn't have been easy for you these past five years, being all alone, no support of any kind, neither financially nor from your family."

Her chin lifted in that stubborn way he'd come to know. "I didn't want my parents' help, Jesse, not as long as they looked at Riley as something to be ashamed of. I'd just as soon take care of her myself, and I have."

She didn't and couldn't tell him of the countless nights she'd lain awake worrying how she was going to put food on the table or gas in the car. Or pay the electricity bill that month.

She'd worked two jobs for as long as she could remember. A regular full-time day job at an office in town, putting Riley in day care. And then another job on weekends at the bookstore in town. In addition to the stress involved in working so much, she'd also missed her daughter desperately, and hated having to leave her. Which was why this job with Tommy was such a blessing.

It was one job that paid more than enough to support them comfortably and she could take Riley with her, where she would be engulfed in a family atmosphere.

Her gratitude and her love toward Tommy knew no bounds.

Forcing a smile, Hannah lifted her head and looked at him. "I don't mean to sound ungrateful, Jesse. I appreciate the fact that Riley and I have been able to live here basically for free for the past five years—except for the horrendous maintenance costs.'' Hannah shrugged. ''But I do what I can, when I can.''

Jesse glanced up at the old house now, quickly appraising it. In addition to the creaking back porch, the windows needed resealing, the entire building needed scraping and painting, the gutters needed to be cleaned and the front porch could do with a little work. ''Do you mean to tell me you do all the maintenance on this big old house yourself?''

She laughed. ''Jesse, I'm a single mother and single mothers do *everything* themselves.''

He frowned. ''Yeah, I know,'' he said quietly, thinking about Grace Garland and how she always did twice as much work as everyone else and still always had time for him.

He glanced at Hannah and realized that like Grace she loved her child and wanted to give her the best life she could. As Grace had done, he thought, watching Hannah in admiration.

Her skin gleamed under the soft porch light, filtering over the blond strands of her hair, making them glitter like flecks of gold. She was still looking at the house that she finally thought of as a home.

''I know I haven't done a very good job of keeping the place up, but I do the best I can when I have the time and the funds. Both of which are rare commodities in a single mother's life,'' she added with a chuckle.

''Hannah-Anna,'' he said quietly, tightening his arm around her and drawing her even closer. ''You are the most incredible woman I've ever met.''

Embarrassed, she laughed. ''I don't think I'm all that

special, Jesse. Honestly. There are millions of single mothers all over the world raising and taking care of their children, working and living and going about their business.'' She shrugged. ''And doing a fine job of it.''

''That doesn't make you any less incredible.'' He hesitated, watching the light play over her face in shadows. ''And there's never been anyone since Riley's father?''

Hannah laughed, then shook her head. ''No Jesse, no one.'' She wasn't certain she could explain this, at least not so it made sense. ''It's very hard to be a single parent, Jesse. You always have to put your child's needs, wants and desires first, as it should be. I never, ever wanted to subject Riley to possibly being rejected by another man.'' She shook her head. ''That's far too painful, especially after being rejected by her own father.''

''I understand,'' he said carefully. ''But what about you? You're a young woman, Hannah. Surely you must have thought about getting married. Or having more children.'' She was a natural mother. It would be a shame for her not to be able to share all the love she had with a husband and more children, particularly considering how much family meant to her.

She let loose a little sigh. ''I'd be lying if I didn't say that I've always wanted more children.'' She laughed. ''Believe it or not, I'd always wanted six. But Jesse, to be honest, I don't have time for a relationship. Riley gets and deserves all of my time. She's my first priority. And after that there are all my other responsibilities. My job. This house.'' She shrugged. ''I just don't have time for a man or a relationship.''

Watching her, he saw the wariness in her eyes again and knew she wasn't telling him the whole truth. There was much more here than her responsibilities to her daughter and the rest of it. Much more. "Earlier tonight you said you'd never felt safe with a man. I think now I understand."

She nodded, not knowing what to say. It was the truth, so she felt silly apologizing for it.

"After what you've been through I can understand your feelings, Hannah. And," he continued, deliberately gentling his voice, "I would also understand it if you felt like you couldn't trust anyone." He blew out a breath, wondering if he was talking about her or himself. "After I first found out that Grace had lied to me, I was devastated. I always thought she was an honorable person, a person of courage and character. And I trusted her implicitly. After her confession, well, darlin', I have to admit, it sort of took away my ability to trust." He shrugged, his large shoulders moving beneath his shirt. "If you can't trust your mother to be honest with you, well, then..." He shook his head. "I didn't know that I'd ever be able to trust anyone again. I guess that was part of why I didn't really want to come here."

"Jesse." She laid a hand on his chest and met his gaze. He was so close she could see her own reflection in his eyes. "I think that's perfectly understandable after what you've been through. But I think you just need to give yourself some time." She smiled at him. "I think if you do, you're going to find that there isn't a family on this planet more worthy of your trust and your love than the Ryans."

He nodded, knowing he wasn't quite ready to talk about this. Not with anyone. Not until he had time to sort out all the feelings and emotions, as well as the memories, that had surfaced the past week. He'd deliberately avoided thinking about everything because whenever he tried to, he was simply, utterly overwhelmed.

Once he was back home in Texas, on familiar ground, he figured he'd be able to sort things out a lot better, and hopefully come to some resolution he could live with.

"Jesse, just give it time."

"I don't have all that much time," he reminded her, making her frown. "But while I am here, Hannah, I appreciate you sharing part of your life and your wonderful daughter with me." It was as sincere a statement as he'd ever made, making him wonder why it seemed so easy to be emotionally open with Hannah. Perhaps it was simply because of their past, shared history.

She had been the first thing he'd remembered. Clearly, she'd been important to him—very important to him—at one time in his life.

In *Jesse Ryan's* life, he corrected, instantly regretting the thought for it brought back all the emotional turmoil that had dogged him for so long.

And after such a wonderful day and evening, he didn't want to spoil it.

His gaze fastened on her mouth and he saw her eyes widen a fraction of a moment before he bent his head and covered her mouth with his.

He felt the jolt of raw desire like a fist to the gut, and tightened his arm around her, dragging her close until the soft warmth of her body was pressed tightly against his.

On a gasp, Hannah's hands went to his chest. She was going to push him away. Going to tell him they couldn't keep doing this. It wasn't good for either of them and it was far too confusing for her.

She was going to tell him. She was sure of it. But her hands slid from his chest around his neck, clinging to him as he deepened the kiss until her head was spinning and her heart thumping.

She moaned softly as he traced her lips with his tongue in a teasing, caressing manner that had her arching against him, silently pleading for more.

Lost in the moment, drowning in her taste, her scent, her touch, Jesse heard the warning echo in his mind. This wasn't a woman to toy with. He'd made her a promise; she'd always be safe with him. And he would honor that promise, especially now that he knew what she'd been through.

He had to remain detached, unemotional. He wasn't staying. He only came to fulfill a deathbed promise.

He had to find his way back...*home.*

He heard the warning ringing soundly in his mind, but the pleasure, need and desire for her smothered them as he held Hannah tighter, wanting, needing, aching for more.

## *Chapter Seven*

"Riley? What on earth are you doing?" Hannah asked with a frown, several mornings later. Hannah glanced up from the checkbook she was trying to balance, to stare at the ceiling.

Riley's bedroom was right over the kitchen table, so every noise, every sound reverberated through the floorboards. Riley was supposed to be cleaning her room, but it sounded as if she was detonating bombs.

"Riley?" Hannah called again, frowning and wondering if she should go investigate. She glanced down at her checkbook, torn. Balancing it was a chore she put off as long as she could because it usually took so much juggling and worrying to get everything paid and the balance...balanced. But now that she had a paycheck that covered all the necessities and a little extra for luxuries, she found it wasn't as daunting a task as before. Still, she didn't like to let it go. She always had to make sure she knew and accounted for every penny to prevent any catastrophes, at least of the financial kind.

"Mama," Riley said a little breathlessly as she came dashing into the room. "I can't find my blue hair ribbons." In her excitement, Riley was almost bouncing out of her shoes. "I have to find my hair ribbons."

Hannah grinned at her daughter. Riley had on a pair of brand-new white tights she'd bought her for the start of school, except her daughter had obviously put them on in a hurry because they were twisted around her knees and sagging at the ankles.

Riley had on one of her new black patent-leather school shoes. The other foot was snuggled into her comfortable old tennis shoe. Her hair was flying loose and her glasses were clouded and slightly askew as well. Hannah pretended not to notice.

"Sweetheart, your blue hair ribbons are on your dresser." She reached out and brushed several golden locks from her daughter's face. "Remember last week when we went shopping for your school clothes? You wore them, and then we put them on your little ribbon stand on the dresser."

"Oh yeah, Mama. I forgot." With a grin, Riley turned, prepared to dash back upstairs, but Hannah caught her arm.

"Whoa, sweetheart." Amusement lit Hannah's face. Riley was obviously in a tizzy about something this morning, and she had a feeling it wasn't over cleaning her room. "Where are you going in such a rush and why are you looking for your blue hair ribbons?" One eyebrow lifted. ''Did you forget that today's Sunday and on Sunday we clean our rooms and do our chores?''

It was a day Hannah had always preserved as family day. No matter what was going on in her life, on Sunday she and Riley had a leisurely breakfast, then spent the morning doing chores. She'd make a big, traditional Sunday dinner and then the two of them would rent movies, make popcorn and settle down in front of the television for the evening. It was a private family time that they both eagerly looked forward to and savored.

''I didn't forget, Mama, honest.'' Riley rubbed her nose with the back of her hand and shoved her slipping glasses up her nose. ''I cleaned my room and did all my chores.'' She grinned at Hannah's skeptical look. ''Honest.'' Riley tugged at her tangled tights, trying unsuccessfully to straighten them. ''I have to go, Mama.'' Riley grinned at her, still tugging at her tights. ''I don't want to be late. I need my ribbons 'cuz I want to look pretty on my date.'' With a grin, Riley dashed out of the room.

*''Date?''* Hannah's brow rose in amusement as she went after her daughter. ''Sweetheart?'' she called as she climbed the stairs. ''Uh, is there something you need to tell me?''

''Riley?'' Hannah stood in the open doorway of her daughter's bedroom. Her daughter had cleaned her room, if you called stuffing everything under the covers and the bed and into the nearest drawer, cleaning it. Every single new outfit and dress that they'd bought for Riley's start of school was crumpled in a pile or strewn haphazardly across the bed. Shaking her head,

Hannah tried not to grin. "I think perhaps we should have a little chat."

"But I'll be late, Mama." Solemn eyes looked up at her as Hannah sat down on Riley's bed. "And that wouldn't be polite. You always say it's not polite to be late."

Did her daughter have to start reciting her mother's wisdom back to her right now? Hannah wondered in amusement.

"I think you can afford a minute or two, sweetheart." She drew Riley close, nestling her between her knees and brushing her long hair out of her eyes. "Now, what's all this about a date?"

Riley beamed, fidgeting from one foot to another. "I have a date with Uncle Jesse."

"A date with Uncle Jesse?" Riley nodded as Hannah reached down and straightened the little girl's tangled tights. "I see. And when did all this happen?"

Riley frowned, then shrugged. "I dunno, Mama." Lifting her head, Riley grinned, shoving her long hair back. "Uncle Jesse said that since I was a big girl now and had a two-wheeler and was gonna go to school, I could probably go on a date with him."

Hannah was struggling not to smile, warmed beyond belief by Jesse's unwavering kindness. "He did, huh?"

"Yep." Riley's head bobbed up and down and then the smile slid off her face. "I forgot to tell you, huh?" Riley said with a guilty look, making Hannah laugh.

"That you did, sweetheart." She pressed a kiss to her Riley's forehead.

"But I can go, huh, can't I, Mama?" Riley pressed

her hands to her mother's cheeks, her eyes pleading. "Can't I?"

"Absolutely, sweetheart," Hannah said, watching as her daughter's shoulders drooped in relief. "So, exactly where are you and Uncle Jesse going?"

Riley shrugged, then chewed her lip. "I don't know." She looked up at her mother earnestly, worry on her face. "I've never been on a date, Mama." She grinned suddenly. "But Uncle Jesse said it would be fun."

Hannah laughed. "I'm sure it will be." She glanced at the clock on Riley's dresser. "Do you know what time Uncle Jesse is coming to pick you up?"

Riley's head bobbed furiously and she turned to look at the clock with a frown. "He said when the big hand was on the twelve and the little hand was on the eleven."

"Eleven this morning?" It was ten-thirty now, which would give her a half hour to help Riley get ready. "Well, sweetheart, I think it's only fair that Mama help you get ready for your first date, don't you?" Hannah stood up, taking her daughter's hand, grateful it would be a few more years before she had to ready her for a real date. "Now, let's find your blue hair ribbons."

"He's here, Mama. He's here." Riley was standing with the front door wide open, her nose pressed against the screen, nearly bouncing out of her new patent-leather shoes. "Uncle Jesse's here."

With a smile, Hannah closed her checkbook, satisfied it was balanced, and went to stand at the front door with her daughter. She couldn't prevent the smile when she saw Jesse climb out of his car. He was carrying a small bouquet of multicolored wildflowers.

"You're here," Riley cried, pushing open the front screen door and bolting down the porch steps to throw herself at Jesse. "It took forever," she said, clinging as she gazed up at him.

"I'm sorry, darlin', but I had to make a few stops first." He laid a hand to Riley's head as his gaze drifted to Hannah. She was standing in the doorway, dressed in a pair of short shorts and a white cotton T-shirt. Her legs and feet were bare, and her hair was pulled up into a ponytail atop her head. She'd never looked more beautiful.

"Uncle Jesse, I told Mama about our date." Riley slid her hand into his and Hannah tried not to think about how right—how perfect—Jesse looked with her daughter. Or how happy her daughter looked with him. The thought brought a little pang to her heart.

"You did?" Jesse went down on his knees so he was eye level with her. "Well, darlin', since I didn't want your mama feeling bad because we were leaving her all alone for a while, I brought her a present from us." He winked at Hannah as he handed Riley the bouquet. "Why don't you go give your mama her present."

"'Kay, Uncle Jesse." Riley skipped back toward the front door and shoved the flowers at her mother. "Here, Mama. It's from us."

"Thank you, sweetheart," Hannah said with a smile, taking a deep whiff of the fragrant blossoms and letting her gaze meet Jesse's. She was touched beyond measure. "And thank you, Jesse," she added quietly. Just looking at him caused her pulse to scramble wildly, and she had an uncommon urge to simply touch him. The thought shook her. She shouldn't be having such thoughts about Jesse and she knew it. He was just being kind, just being a friend. There was absolutely nothing more to it. Couldn't be more to it. Not for her. And certainly not for him. "Would you like to come in? Have some coffee?"

Jesse shook his head, giving Riley's hand a gentle squeeze. "Thanks, darlin', but me and Miss Riley here have plans." He glanced down at Riley and gave her little hand a quick, gentle squeeze. "Don't we, darlin'?"

"Yep." Riley started tugging Jesse's hand toward the car. "Could we go now, Uncle Jesse? I've been ready forever." She tugged him along as he turned back to Hannah.

"We'll be back around four," Jesse called to her, digging in his jeans pocket for his keys. "Don't worry," he said when he saw her chewing her lip. "I promise I'll take very good care of her."

She nodded, still worrying her lip. She felt foolish telling him that she couldn't help but worry. In the five years since Riley's birth, her daughter had never gone off alone with anyone. Not anyone.

Hannah's gaze shifted to Riley, wondering if she was feeling any distress or separation anxiety. Hannah couldn't help but smile. Her daughter looked as if she couldn't wait to get going, and didn't seem particularly bothered by the fact that she was going off alone with someone other than her mother for the first time.

"Jesse, would you like to stay for dinner?" Hannah called impulsively, realizing she and Riley had never shared their special day or Sunday dinner with anyone before.

Two very new things in one day. For a women who prided herself on calm, careful stability, and always thought everything through twice, then thought it through again, she was sure being carefree today, she thought in amusement.

There was just something about Jesse that seemed to make her forget her usual calm, careful resolve.

"We'll bring dinner back with us," Jesse called with a wink. He opened the door and helped Riley inside the car, secured her seat belt tightly, then double-checked it. When he shut the door and started to round the car, he turned back to Hannah. "You've got a few hours to yourself, Hannah. Try to do something fun," he said with a mischievous smile. "Something just for you, darlin'." He blew her a kiss that sent a heated shiver over her as if he'd actually kissed her and not been standing five feet away. "You deserve a day off." With a wave, he climbed into the car, started the engine and drove off. Riley, her nose pressed against the window, waved frantically, a wide grin of happiness on her face.

Hannah stood there for a long moment, the bouquet still in her hands, touched almost to tears, finally understanding Jesse's "date" with her daughter.

Jesse was giving her a day off, some time to herself with no responsibilities or worries. She pressed the flowers to her nose and couldn't prevent the warmth that spread through her from settling in her wary heart at his kindness, his caring.

He was, she decided, an incredible man.

And he'd chosen to spend the day with her daughter, giving Riley the benefit of his time and attention. Making her one very happy little girl.

Hannah's smile widened and the warmth spread deeper. Slowly, she shut the front door, then locked it, before making her way to the kitchen to put the flowers into a vase.

She couldn't remember a time when she was all alone and had hours stretching ahead of her with nothing to do, no responsibilities and nothing tugging at her time.

With a happy sigh, Hannah realized she had almost five long, lovely hours to do anything she wanted.

Jesse, she thought, sniffing the flowers one last time before arranging them in a vase, what on earth are you doing to my defenses?

More importantly, what on earth was he doing to her scarred and wary heart?

She wasn't going to waste a perfectly lovely day worrying. Instead, she planned to do exactly what Jesse had suggested; she was going to do something fun.

Feeling a little bit decadent, Hannah poured herself a large glass of iced cola, then went into the pantry and grabbed a bag of potato chips. Laughing at her own foolishness, she walked into the living room, pausing at the bookcase. She couldn't remember the last time she actually had the time to sit down and just read a book. To get lost in another world for a moment, a world where she was just a casual observer with no responsibilities.

Spotting the newest Nora Roberts novel she'd been dying to read, Hannah grabbed it, then set down her soda before sinking into a chair. With another happy sigh, she tucked her legs under her, opened the bag of chips and the book, then leaned back and began to read.

"And then, Mama, the elephant gave a big loud snort and water came squirting out of his nose. All over everything." Riley covered her mouth and collapsed on the blanket in a fit of giggles, startling a flock of birds in a tree overhead.

"It sounds like you had a wonderful time at the zoo," Hannah said with a laugh, rubbing a hand across her daughter's head. "But I think you'd better eat something." Hannah reached across the blanket and pulled a piece of fried chicken out of the basket Jesse and Riley had brought back with them, and handed it to her daughter.

When Riley and Jesse had returned just a little over half an hour ago, she'd just finished her book and had been wiping a tear from her eye, wishing her life was more like one of the heroines in a book—with a happily-ever-after.

The sight of her daughter standing in the doorway beaming, exhausted and totally disheveled, had brought Hannah back to reality. Riley had a lime-green mustache from the snow cone she'd had, as well as a few stains on her new blue school dress from using it as a napkin. She'd lost one of her blue ribbons somewhere along the way, and her new patent-leather shoes were scuffed, but Riley had never looked happier, warming Hannah's heart.

When Jesse had pulled a large box of fried chicken with all the fixings from the back seat of his car, they'd decided to have a picnic in the backyard.

Jesse had offered to set things up for their outdoor picnic, so Hannah went inside to give Riley a bath and change her into her pajamas, knowing her daughter was about to collapse.

Now, sitting on the blanket, under the warmth of the low setting sun, listening to her daughter recall her day, Hannah couldn't help but be struck by how normal it all seemed.

So unbelievably normal.

Like a family, she thought. A real family. Oh, they'd been their own family, just the two of them, but adding Jesse, adding a man to the equation, seemed to change things substantially. And Hannah wasn't sure how comfortable she was with the situation, especially knowing Jesse was leaving and Riley was growing more and more attached to him.

As was Hannah.

They were like a family, she thought again, trying to curb the deep pang of longing that had blossomed earlier today when she had watched Jesse and Riley leave together.

They'd looked like a father and daughter going out on an outing together. Something she'd always wanted but had never been able to give her daughter.

Watching Riley and the way she seemed to blossom under Jesse's attention and affection made Hannah realize that as much as she'd tried to be both mother and father to her precious daughter, it just wasn't possible.

Riley was desperately in need of male attention and affection. It was so obvious from the way she responded and reacted to Jesse, Hannah could scarcely believe she hadn't been more aware of it before this.

Perhaps because until now all the Ryan men had filled in the gap and done a very good job of making Riley feel very much a part of their family. But it wasn't until this very moment that Hannah realized how much her daughter had missed having a father of her own.

Hannah glanced away, unaware that Jesse was watching her intently. She had accepted full responsibility for being a single parent, but until now she hadn't realized that perhaps her own pride and her own past was hurting her daughter.

''You all right, darlin'?'' Jesse asked quietly, laying his hand over hers. With a forced smile, she turned to him, aware that Riley was sitting between them.

''Fine, Jesse.'' She forced her smile wider. ''Just fine.''

''You haven't eaten much.'' Cocking his head, he studied her, sliding a hand to her cheek. It was warm from the warmth of the sun. ''Don't you like fried chicken?'' he asked in a tone of voice that made her laugh.

''You make it sound like not liking fried chicken is a national offense.''

He laughed, and the sound floated on the quiet air. ''Darlin', where I come from it is.'' His eyebrows drew together. "If you'd like, I can run out and get you something else."

She squeezed his hand, so warm and gentle under hers. "No thanks, Jesse. I love fried chicken actually." She glanced at Riley who was busy munching on a chicken leg. Her daughter's eyes were drooping. Riley was utterly exhausted. "I guess I'm just not very hungry."

"Something troubling you?" he asked in concern, and she shook her head.

"No, not really." Slowly, she withdrew her hand from his, knowing it would be easier to think if she wasn't touching him.

"Well now, darlin', there's no. And then there's not really," he said with a wiggle of his eyebrows. "Seems to me they're two different things."

"Uncle Jesse?" Riley tugged on his shirt, interrupting their conversation. "Should we tell Mama about the surprise now?"

Hannah's mother's alarm went off and she lifted an eyebrow, encompassing both Jesse and her daughter with one glance.

"Surprise?" she asked with a bit of nervousness, making Jesse grin.

"You said we had to wait to tell Mama until she had a full stomach. Is she full now?" Riley asked as Jesse grabbed the little girl and tumbled her into his lap.

"I imagine she is," Jesse said, bending to nuzzle Riley's neck, which made her giggle.

*"A full stomach?"* Hannah repeated in concern, pressing a hand to her forehead. "And exactly what

kind of surprise would have to wait until I had a full stomach?'' She was almost certain whatever it was, she didn't want to know, not if the matching mischievous grins Jesse and Riley were wearing was any indication.

''Guess what, Mama?''

''Oh Lord,'' Hannah muttered, hanging her head, feeling as if the other shoe—one Jesse had deliberately filled with cement—was about to drop. ''What, darling?'' she asked, lifting her head and forcing a smile.

''Ditka's going to be a daddy.''

Hannah blinked. Several times. Then her confused gaze went from Riley to Jesse then back again. ''This is what you had to tell me on a full stomach?'' she asked in confusion. ''That Timmy and Terry's dog is going to be a father?''

''Not...exactly,'' Jesse began slowly, sharing a look with Riley. They both started giggling, making Hannah even more nervous.

''Then what...*exactly?*'' Hannah asked carefully, still looking from one to the other.

''Remember what you said, Mama? You said that we had to wait a while to talk about getting me a puppy and it's been a while. A *real long* while,'' Riley pointed out with a dramatic roll of her eyes. ''So could I have one, Mama, huh? Please?'' Riley looked at her expectantly, tongue caught between her missing front teeth, a look of pure pleading in her eyes.

Hannah merely groaned. ''Is Ditka really having puppies?'' she asked Jesse, who nodded his head slowly. ''Traitor,'' she muttered under her breath, making him laugh. He caught her with his free arm, dragging her close.

Off balance, she fell against him, felt the hard wall of his chest, the comfort of his arm, the warmth of his breath, and felt her heart speed up.

"Now, Hannah-Anna, don't tell me you wouldn't love to have a little puppy," he whispered. He was so close, she could feel a shiver race over and down her neck, starting an ache low and deep in her belly. It annoyed her to know she responded so quickly, so readily to him. She thought she was immune to this kind of feminine frivolity. She was a mother with enormous responsibilities and shouldn't be reacting like a schoolgirl in the throes of her first crush.

Still scowling, Hannah glanced up at him and nearly growled. "Jesse, if I wanted to walk or feed something during the night, I'd have had another baby."

"Mama, can I have a brother or sister now, too?" Riley asked hopefully, her face gleaming with excitement, making Hannah groan again. She shot Jesse a lethal look. In spite of his hand in this ploy, he managed to look perfectly innocent.

Struggling free of him, Hannah straightened her clothes and tried to gather her composure. "Now, Riley, let's take one thing at a time." Hannah dragged her hands through her hair, trying to figure a way out of this. "Remember what I said about a baby brother or sister?" She spoke directly to her daughter, trying to ignore Jesse's obvious amusement over how she was going to explain the facts of life—or rather *her* life—to her daughter.

Riley's head bobbed and the corners of her mouth drooped in disappointment. "That we can't have a baby brother or sister because we can't stay home to take care of it and stuff, right?'' Riley said with a heavy sigh.

''Is that the real reason, Hannah-Anna?'' Jesse asked with a wiggle of his eyebrows, causing Hannah to whack him on the arm.

''I don't need any help here, Jesse,'' she said, giving him a look. ''I think you've helped more than enough for one day.''

''Anytime, darlin','' he said with a grin, giving a pretend yelp when she whacked him again, loving the way her eyes were sparkling. Her day off had obviously done her a world of good. He hadn't seen her look this carefree or relaxed since he'd arrived. It made his heart ache to look at her, starting a strange longing deep inside, a longing he didn't understand. But with all the other emotions swirling around inside, he didn't worry too much about this one.

''Now, sweetheart.'' Hannah took a breath as Riley snuggled deeper into Jesse's lap, resting her head on his shoulder. ''You know we can't have a baby brother or sister for you,'' Hannah said, expecting the same pout and plea she always got from her disappointed daughter.

''But what about a puppy, Mama?'' Rubbing her tired eyes with a fist, Riley tried unsuccessfully to stifle a yawn. ''Uncle Jesse said—''

''Uncle Jesse, again,'' Hannah muttered, giving him another look. He merely grinned, reaching out to ruffle her hair. She tried to glare at him, but simply couldn't manage it.

''But Mama, Uncle Jesse said we could leave my puppy at his house 'cuz it will be too little to leave its mommy. And then when it's big enough, we could bring it home.''

''But Riley—''

''Hannah.'' Jesse's touch on her hand stopped her. ''Natalie is home all day, every day with the twins. She offered to keep the puppy there until it's weaned, and train it along with the others before you bring it home.'' Jesse grinned that heartbreaking grin, the one she never seemed to be able to resist. ''That way Riley will be able to see it every day when you go to work, spend time with it, play with it and get accustomed to taking care of it.''

''I'll take care of it. Honest, Mama.'' Riley was on her knees, hands pressed together as if in prayer, ready to beg. ''Please, Mama? Pul-lease?''

''Riley, wait.'' She held up her hand and tried to sort out her thoughts. ''Let me talk to Uncle Jesse for a minute.'' Stunned by the generosity of Natalie's offer, Hannah could only stare at him. ''I can't believe Natalie made such a generous offer. Jesse, that's not really fair to her. I mean I have a lot of responsibility, but she has two sets of twins to take care of as well as a husband, two dogs and an assortment of other pets.''

Jesse shrugged his massive shoulders. ''That's what I said. But Natalie merely laughed and said she'd be glad to do it just to know she'd have a home for at least one of the pups.''

''So can I have a puppy, Mama? Please?'' Riley reached out and hooked an arm around Hannah's neck. ''I promise I'll take care of it.''

''It will be a good way to teach her responsibility,

Hannah, and it will also keep her company. I think it would be wonderful for her.''

With two pairs of pleading eyes on hers, Hannah felt her resolve cave in. Torn, she thought of every single reason why having a new puppy was not only not practical but downright illogical. She barely had enough time to take care of all of her responsibilities now. Where on earth would she find the time to take care of a puppy as well? She hadn't a clue. She was about to decline, to go into a lengthy explanation of all the reasons why it just wasn't feasible, but then she looked at her daughter's face. And her resolve faltered as her heart melted.

''I know I'm going to regret this,'' she muttered, giving Jesse another look.

''I can have it?'' Riley turned to Jesse, her eyes sparkling in excitement. ''Does that mean I can have one?''

''It does indeed, darlin'.'' Jesse almost fell backward as Riley threw herself at him, winding her arms around his neck and bouncing up and down.

''Thank you, Uncle Jesse. Thank you.'' She planted wet, sloppy kisses all over his face. ''Thank you.''

''Hey, what about me?'' Hannah asked with a grin. ''Don't I get any kisses or any thanks?''

Riley lunged at her, draping herself over her mother and hugging her tight. ''Thank you, Mama.'' She planted wet kisses all over Hannah's face as well. ''Thank you, thank you. I promise I'll take good care of it. Honest.''

Hannah nodded, knowing that a five-year-old's promises were about as good as the time it took to say them. She sighed. So she'd find some extra time somewhere to take care of the puppy. It was worth it if it made her daughter this happy.

''Okay, now that we've got that settled.'' Hannah drew back and looked at her child. ''Sweetheart, I want you to remember this is a real living creature with feelings and needs. He's a baby really and he'll need you to take care of him. He'll be depending on you for everything. His food. His safety. His well-being.''

''Like you take care of me, Mama?''

Hannah grinned. ''Yes, sweetheart, like I take care of you.'' She pressed a kiss to her daughter's freckled nose. ''It's a very big responsibility, honey.''

''I know, Mama, and I could do it. I'm big enough. Honest.''

''I'm sure you will.'' Hannah sighed, wondering how on earth one man and a five-year-old had bushwhacked her. She didn't know, but looking at the joy on her daughter's face, it really didn't matter. ''Now, you have a very big day tomorrow, young lady—''

''Tomorrow's my first day of school, Uncle Jesse.''

''Yes, darlin', I know.''

''And I get to ride on a bus and everything.'' Riley bit her lower lip and glanced away. ''But I'm not afraid.''

Jesse didn't have to hear the waver in Riley's voice to know she was terrified. '''Course you're not, darlin',' Jesse said, scooping her into his arms and planting her on his hip as he stood up. ''There's nothing to be afraid of.'' He jiggled her as he started walking toward the back door with her. ''You're going to learn so many new and fun things, meet so many new friends. When you come home you can tell your mama and me all about your day, how does that sound?"

Riley grinned, winding her arm around Jesse and laying her head down on his shoulder. "Uncle Jesse, I'll tell you everything." Riley shoved her glasses up. "And maybe I could even draw you a picture."

"Why, that would be wonderful, darlin'. Just wonderful."

"Uncle Jesse, will you come tuck me in?"

"Sure, darlin'." He glanced back at Hannah. "You coming?"

Hannah followed, listening, watching, her heart caught in her throat. Jesse had said he'd be here tomorrow when Riley came home from school.

And her daughter was eagerly looking forward to it, as was she, Hannah realized. But Jesse wasn't always going to be there when Riley came home from school. She knew that. But looking at her little girl's face, so open, so filled with love, Hannah realized that her daughter didn't.

And when that day came, when Jesse wasn't there when Riley came home, when Jesse was back home in Texas, what would happen to Riley and the love and adoration she'd so freely and openly given to Jesse?

Hannah couldn't bear to even think about that day.

Riley was only five and didn't understand the rules of life; didn't understand that just wanting something—loving someone—didn't make things turn out all right.

Hannah knew it better than anyone, and had vowed to protect herself from ever being so naive again.

With a sigh, Hannah realized she couldn't deny that her feelings for Jesse went beyond friendship. Up until now she hadn't been able to acknowledge her own feelings, let alone accept them.

But now, watching him with her daughter, knowing he was leaving, knowing he would leave both her and Riley devastated, Hannah realized she had to do something.

Perhaps it was too late to rescue her own heart.

But she had to protect her daughter's.

She was going to have to talk to him, she realized. She was going to have to tell him that as much as she loved having him spend time with her and Riley, as much as loved his presence, his touch, she didn't think it was a good idea for him to spend any more time with them simply because of the situation.

He was leaving, there was no doubt about that. He'd reiterated that many times so there would be no doubt. She had no choice now but to tell him that he couldn't spend so much time with Riley. Or with her.

The thought made Hannah's wary heart ache in a way that almost brought on a physical pain unlike anything in memory. Watching Jesse with her daughter she realized that she was going to have to hurt the two people she cared about most in the world, and in the end, hurt herself as well.

## *Chapter Eight*

Tommy glanced up from his morning newspaper. "Aye, Jesse, my boy, you're up early," he said with a slight frown as Jesse wandered into the kitchen.

"I couldn't sleep," Jesse admitted with a shrug, rubbing his tired, bleary eyes.

Setting his coffee cup down, Tommy carefully looked at his grandson.

"Something troubling you, lad?" He'd not pushed the boy, letting him adjust at his own pace, feeling that would be best if the lad was ever going to feel comfortable with the clan and his place in it.

Jesse shrugged, grabbed a coffee mug from the cabinet and poured himself some coffee, turning to Tommy with a sheepish grin.

"It's Riley's first day of school," he admitted with another shrug of his shoulders. "I guess I'm as nervous as she is,'' he said with a chuckle as he sat down at the kitchen table and took a sip of his coffee.

''Aye,'' Tommy said with a nod and understanding smile. ''Firsts are always a time for worry, Jesse.'' He glanced at his grandson. ''No matter your age, nerves flutter the first time you do anything.''

Jesse sipped his coffee, wondering if Tommy was only talking about Riley. Or about him as well. Obviously he'd been nervous coming here for the first time, but it was only natural, he supposed, considering the circumstances.

''But I'm sure the little lass will do fine.'' Tommy picked up the cigar smoldering in the ashtray and took a puff. ''You know, lad, Hannah's done a fine, fine job with her little girl.'' Tommy grinned as he took a sip of coffee. ''Hannah's like my own daughter, Jesse. Had I had a daughter, I would have wanted her to be just like Hannah. She's a strong woman with a heart as big as the ocean.'' Tommy chuckled. ''And as proud and loyal as any of the Ryan clan, with a strong stubborn streak in the way that women have.'' Tommy winked at him. ''If you know what I mean.''

Jesse laughed. He thought about Hannah for a moment, and couldn't help the smile that filtered over his face. ''Hannah has that little feminine stubborn streak you're talking about, I reckon.''

''Aye, I agree, lad.'' Tommy hesitated, puffing thoughtfully on his cigar. ''Being a single mother, Jesse, why, it's a difficult chore at best. It's not easy raising a child alone.''

''I know,'' Jesse said, still thinking about Hannah

and how incredible she was. In some ways she reminded him of Grace Garland in her devotion to Riley.

Leaning forward, Tommy laid a hand on his grandson's arm. He'd not spoken to the boy about the woman who'd raised him as her own. He felt the lad needed some time to get used to the clan again, to find his footing and his proper place. And Tommy wasn't certain yet that the lad had done that. But still, he felt the need to speak of things now.

''Jesse, in spite of what you think, I'm heartily indebted to Grace Garland for taking care of you for so many years.'' Stunned by the abrupt change in subject, Jesse's gaze shifted to Tommy's. ''A woman alone, I'm sure it wasn't an easy time for her. I was sorry to hear of her passing, son. Truly. And I want you to know I understand the love and loyalty you feel toward her.'' Tommy smiled at Jesse's look of surprise. ''Without her, who knows how things would have turned out.'' Tommy hesitated, then shrugged. ''And I hope, lad, you know that coming back here to your clan, your family, well, it has nothing to do with the love you have for Grace Garland. Aye, nothing at all. The love in your heart is that of a son for a mother, as it should be,'' Tommy said. ''She *was* your mother during the years it most mattered.'' Tommy hesitated, watching his grandson carefully. ''But love is a funny thing, Jesse, as is loyalty. It's like when you have a second child. You can't possibly imagine loving another wee one as much as you love the first, and you wonder at times how you'll do it, fearing you'll be unfair to the new addition.'' Tommy grinned. ''But aye, when that new babe is born, it's as if the love in your heart grows and multiplies so there's always plenty enough to go around.''

Jesse searched his grandfather's eyes. ''Tommy, I don't reckon I'm sure what you're saying,'' he admitted, wanting, needing to understand.

Tommy blew out a breath, then set his cigar in the ashtray so he could meet his grandson's intense gaze. He laid his hands over Jesse's. ''What I'm saying, lad, is not to feel guilty for loving Grace Garland, or for feeling loyalty toward her. It's a natural thing, considering. And don't think that if you love her, you can't love us.'' Tommy shrugged again. ''We're all your family, Jesse. All of us. Me, Grace Garland, your brothers. A family isn't just about blood ties, lad. Look at Hannah. I couldn't love her more if she were my blood. Love is what makes a family, Jesse, my boy. And I would never want you to forsake your feelings for Grace because of us. Nay, that's not expected at all,'' Tommy said with a firm shake of his head. ''It's not a question of choosing one over the other, lad, or loving one over the other, but more a question of simply sharing your love and your loyalty with all those who love you.''

Jesse couldn't hide his surprise. He'd been absolutely certain that by coming here he would somehow be forced to distance himself from the only mother he'd ever known or remembered. He knew that he could never do that, not without feeling disloyal, something which he didn't think he could bear.

Now Tommy was telling him it was okay to keep his memories and his love of his mother and yet still be a Ryan.

He could be exactly who he needed to be, whoever he truly was, without forsaking his feelings for anyone.

He felt a burden lift off his aching heart and every muscle in his body, every muscle that had been tensed since he began this journey, finally, blissfully relaxed. The ache he'd carried in his heart from the moment Grace had told him the truth seemed to heal over. Yes, there were still scars, there probably always would be, but they would heal as well he knew.

In time. As Hannah had told him. He just needed to give things time.

"Thanks, Tommy," Jesse said, his voice husky with emotion. "I...I want you to know how much that means to me. Love and loyalty aren't just words to me, but part of me, like the blood running through my veins. And for whatever Grace Garland did or didn't do, she loved me more than anything in the world. And I know that. I always knew it. In her heart I was her son."

"And she was your mother, lad. I understand that." Tommy's smile was wistful. "There's something fierce about a mother's love, and a mother isn't only one who gives birth, lad. Nay, a mother is one who loves and cares for a child without selfishness, who does what's best for the babe no matter what the situation." He shrugged. "Grace Garland did what she thought was best."

"You're not angry with her?" Jesse asked in surprise.

Tommy's smile was slow. "Angry? Nay, lad. I can't say that anger's the right word. Grateful she took care of you, raised you as she did. She had other choices, lad. Good choices and bad choices, but she chose the only one she could live with, the one that was best for her. It's all each of us can expect from ourselves, and when we make our choices, aye, we've got to live with them. And I'll be eternally grateful that she made the choice she did.'' Tommy shook his head. ''If she'd chosen not to keep you, son, the outcome could have been far different had you been left with that scoundrel brother of hers. You could have been in a great deal of danger, but Grace loved you enough to protect you, to keep you safe, to love and raise you as her own. So how could I be angry?'' Tommy patted Jesse's hand. ''Nothing is more important than family, Jesse. Nothing.'' Tommy smiled, then cocked his head to look at his grandson. ''Now, if I can pry into my grandson's life...?''

Jesse laughed, then sipped his coffee, feeling more at ease than he had since he'd left Texas. ''Pry away, Tommy.''

Taking a puff on his cigar, Tommy was thoughtful before turning to Jesse. ''So how is it you've never married, lad? Never had a family of your own?''

Jesse laughed, fingering his coffee mug. ''Guess I didn't really have time and I guess I just haven't met the right woman.'' He didn't think it necessary to go into the problem he had about letting people get emotionally close to him. Tommy was so open, so loving, he wasn't sure the old man would be able to understand.

''’Twas a time I felt as if I'd never marry, either,'' Tommy said softly, watching Jesse through a haze of cigar smoke.

"You?" Jesse laughed, then shook his head. "I have a hard time imagining you not married, Tommy, considering the way you feel about family." Tommy's feelings had been quite clear in each and every one of his letters, as well as during every conversation they'd had since he'd arrived.

"Aye, yes, boy, but you see, it's not just marrying a lass, son, it's finding the *right* lass that makes all the difference." Tommy glanced up at his grandson, his coffee forgotten for the moment. "Now take Hannah for instance. I thought for certain she and one of your brothers would end up together." Tommy laughed. "In fact, I would have wagered a good portion of my wealth on it. And I would have lost," he admitted with a chuckle.

Jesse glanced up at his grandfather, wondering why he felt a stab of jealousy at the thought of Hannah with another man. Even if it was one of his own brothers.

Thoughtfully, Tommy pulled out his slim gold lighter and relit his cigar. "But I'm afraid, lad, there was no chemistry there except for the brotherly kind." Eyes twinkling, he smiled at Jesse. "And I'm afraid, for a wife or a marriage, that won't do."

Curious, Jesse listened to his grandfather thoughtfully. Tommy let out a sigh. "It's a shame Hannah's not met the right man and married, for the lass was meant for family." Tommy glanced up, a quick grin on his lips. "It's not been for lack of interest though, I can tell you that," he added with a laugh, causing Jesse to feel another, stronger spurt of jealousy. "Half the men in this county have shown an interest, but Hannah's rebuffed them all." Tommy shook his head.

"Something happened years ago that frightened the lass terribly, I'm afraid. And when a woman's had a disappointment from a man, it tends to make her as shy and scared as a newborn filly." Lifting his coffee, which was now cold, Tommy sipped carefully. "'Tis a shame that such a fine lass hasn't found her match yet. For it would be a lucky man to claim Hannah's heart."

"What's going on?" Jake asked, stumbling bleary-eyed through the back door. He headed for an empty chair and dropped down into it, scrubbing his hands over his face and wishing for a few more hours of sleep.

"It's Riley's first day of school," Jesse said, getting up to pour Jake a mug of coffee, then sliding it across the table to him. He refilled his own cup as he turned with a shrug. "I couldn't sleep."

With a nod of understanding, Jake lifted a hand in gratitude, then closed his eyes and sipped quietly, letting out a healthy sigh of relief as the caffeine poured through his system, jolting him into consciousness.

"Caffeine," Jake muttered. "Definitely gets the heart going." He glanced up at Jesse feeling more awake and more human. "Riley's first day of school, huh?" He grinned. "I've got a few more years to go for that."

Jesse shrugged. "I figured I'd go over and see her off. Maybe give Hannah some moral support."

"Sounds like a fine plan to me," Tommy said with a smile.

"Tommy?" Jesse frowned a bit. "Do you by chance have any tools I can borrow?"

''Tools?'' Tommy spread his hands out. ''On a spread this size, lad, we've got enough tools to stock a major city hardware store, if Jared is to be believed.'' He grinned. ''Anything here is yours, lad, to do with what you want.''

''Planning on doing some work?'' Jake asked, getting up to refill his coffee.

''Morning,'' Jared mumbled, coming into the kitchen, a fussy baby nestled on his hip. Without a word, he headed toward the coffeepot, pouring himself a cup, then automatically reached for a teething biscuit in a jar for his son. J.J. was teething and fussy as an old cow.

Smiling in sympathy, Jesse pulled out a chair for Jared, which he gratefully sank into.

''Morning,'' Josh said cheerfully as he came in the back door, looking fresh and crisp in a three-piece gray suit and a blindingly white dress shirt.

Jake scowled at him and sat down. ''Do you have to be so chipper in the morning?'' he growled, taking in his brother's clothing. ''And how can you smile when you've got a noose tied around your neck every morning?''

''Well, good morning to you, too,'' Josh said, giving Jake a whack on the back of the head as he went to pour his own cup of coffee. He dragged out a chair and sat down at the table. It had become a ritual since Jesse had arrived for all of them to head to Tommy's for coffee in the morning.

''So what's everybody up to today?'' Josh asked, taking a sip of his coffee.

''Same as always,'' Jared muttered, picking up the

teething biscuit J.J. had let fly across the kitchen. "Chores. And more chores," he said with a laugh. "I've got the vet coming this afternoon to check on that new heifer. A fence along the south perimeter is down, and then there're the repairs to the henhouse." Jared shrugged, then grinned, handing his son back his teething biscuit. "The usual, like I said."

Jake drained his coffee cup, then sighed. "I've got another day of heavy negotiations with this lawyer over in Lawford. He's representing the owner of a piece of prime land that I think would make a fine addition to our holdings." Jake blew out a breath. "But they're hanging tough."

Josh frowned. "Jake, haven't you been working on that for weeks?"

Jake nodded. "Like I said, another day of heavy negotiations."

"Well, if you need some help or reinforcements, let me know." Josh hunched forward, wrapping his hands around his coffee mug. "I've got to meet with the prospective tenants of the old Saddle Falls movie theater. Someone's finally interested in leasing the building, so I set up a meeting for later this morning." He frowned. "Then I've got to get all the leases prepared. All the tenants who rent offices in the hotel building are coming up for renewal. So I've got a full day as well." Josh looked at Jesse. "So what do you have planned for the day?"

"Well, I was just asking Tommy if he had some tools I could borrow. I thought I'd go over and do some work on Hannah's house. It's sorely in need of some maintenance, and I know she doesn't have the time, the tools or the money to take care of it.'' Jesse shrugged. ''So as long as I've got some free time, I thought I'd put it to good use.''

''You need some help?'' Jake asked with a frown.

''Or some company?'' Jared offered.

''Or both?'' Josh inquired.

Jesse grinned, stunned and surprised by the generous offers. All of them had their own busy schedules today, yet they thought nothing of offering their assistance.

So this is what a family did, Jesse thought, realizing that he didn't feel quite so solitary. As if everything rested on his shoulders alone. Not that he minded, he had always handled responsibility well. But then again, he'd had no choice since there'd been no other male around to help with it.

''You all have your own agendas today,'' Jesse said with a smile. ''But I do appreciate the offers.''

Jake, Jared and Josh exchanged looks, then Jake stood up, speaking for them all. ''Well, Jesse, tell you what. How about we take care of our business this morning.'' Jake pushed his chair in, prepared to get going. ''Then we'll run over to Hannah's this afternoon and give you a hand. What do you say?''

''I'd like that,'' he said with a smile, feeling nearly overwhelmed by the emotions that rushed through him, over him. ''Thanks, guys.''

Standing at the curb, waiting for the school bus, holding tightly to Riley's hand, Hannah struggled to hide her emotions. She couldn't very well expect her daughter to be brave if she was blubbering like a baby.

''Now, sweetheart,'' she said, hoping her voice was

calm. ''Remember, try not to lose your schoolbag.'' As a precaution, Hannah adjusted the bright red straps higher on her daughter's shoulders. ''I put a snack in there for recess.''

''What's recess, Mama?'' Riley asked, glancing up at her mother and clinging tightly to her hand.

Hannah smiled. ''Remember, honey, when we went to visit your school and met your teacher? She told you that about halfway through the morning you and all your classmates could go outside and play. That's recess and when you should eat your snack.''

''On the playground, right? We get to go on the playground?''

''That's right, sweetheart. And remember what I said about being careful?'' She didn't want to scare her daughter, but she also wanted Riley to be cautious. ''Don't go on anything that's too big for you, okay? You know what Mama lets you go on, sweetheart.''

'''Kay, Mama.'' Craning her neck, Riley stared down the empty street. ''Mama, what if the bus doesn't come now? Or what if they forget about me after school?'' Hannah could hear the fear trembling in her daughter's voice and it nearly broke her heart.

''Oh, sweetheart.'' Hannah went down on her knees and hugged her child. ''The bus will come. Promise. And if it doesn't, Mama will drive you to school.'' She adjusted the ribbons in Riley's pigtails. ''And I don't want you to worry that the bus will forget about you after school, either. If that ever happens, I don't want you to worry, okay? All you have to do is go back inside the school and find your teacher or another adult.

Tell them you missed the bus and they'll call Mama and I'll come and get you. Do you understand?''

Riley nodded, then glanced up at the sound of a horn honking. ''Look, Mama, it's Uncle Jesse!'' Riley started bouncing and waving as Jesse's SUV approached and pulled to a stop right in front of the driveway.

''Well now, darlin', don't you look pretty this morning?'' Jesse said, walking toward Riley and holding something behind his back.

''I have a new dress,'' Riley said, pulling out the hem and twirling around for him to see.

He chuckled at her charm, feeling sorry for the men of her generation. They wouldn't stand a chance. ''And it's a mite pretty dress as well.'' He glanced at Hannah, saw the fear shimmering in her eyes and slipped his hand in hers, giving her a reassuring squeeze.

''What's behind your back, Uncle Jesse?'' Riley asked, trying to peek around him.

''This?'' With a grin, he pulled his hand from behind his back. ''This, Miss Riley, is Snoofus. He was mine when I was a little boy.'' He showed her the mangled one-eared dog that had been sitting on his bed for more than twenty years. ''When I was just a little guy, like you, my father gave me Snoofus. He was my first and best friend. Anytime I was scared, Snoofus protected me. As long as he was with me, I was never, ever scared. Not of anything,'' he said solemnly, watching her eyes widen in awe.

''Really?'' Riley asked, eyes wide as saucers. ''Can...can...I touch him?'' she asked reverently, clearly already in love as she lifted a hand, afraid to touch the stuffed dog.

"Touch him?" Jesse grinned at her. "Why, darlin', you can do better than that. Snoofus has been lonely lately since I haven't had much time to spend with him, so I was hoping maybe you could take him along to school with you."

"Snoofus could come with me?" Riley's eyes gleamed wider in expectation and hope. "Really?"

"Scout's honor," Jesse said, holding up two fingers to show his sincerity. "You can keep him company and introduce him to all your new friends." Jesse bent down and tucked the dog securely into Riley's arms. "And as long as you've got him with you, you won't be scared. Not of anything. I promise. Snoofus will always keep you safe, darlin'."

Eyes wide and shining, Riley couldn't stop staring at her new friend, devotedly touching his one ear, his slightly mangled eye, his mended paw. "He's so pretty," she said, glancing up at her mother. "Isn't he, Mama?"

Hannah squeezed Jesse's hand in thanks. "Very pretty, sweetheart." She had to swallow to speak around the lump in her throat.

"Here comes the bus," Riley said, her voice a bit shaky as she clung tighter to her mother's hand and the one-eared dog.

Hannah glanced down the road and saw the bright yellow vehicle rumbling down the road and felt her stomach roll over. She had a wild urge to grab Riley, run in the house and hide under the bed. As irrational as the thought was, at the moment, letting her precious child go off alone without her, to a strange place, on a strange vehicle, was far more intimidating and frightening then anything in memory.

"Now, Miss Riley, before you head off on your big adventure, can I have a kiss?" Jesse asked with a grin.

Riley bobbed her head, let go of her mother's hand and stepped close to Jesse. "Thank you, Uncle Jesse."

He went down on his knees so he was eye level with her. "You're welcome, darlin'." He slid his hands to her tiny waist and pressed a kiss to her forehead.

"Uncle Jesse?" Riley whispered, glancing up at her mother. "I think Mama's sad."

Jesse glanced up at Hannah, then smiled. "Not sad, darlin'. I think she's just jealous because you get to go have all the fun, isn't that right, Hannah-Anna," he prompted, giving Hannah a warning look.

She forced herself to relax, to smile so that she wouldn't frighten her daughter. "That's right, sweetheart."

"Uncle Jesse, will you keep Mama company while I'm gone?" Riley whispered, leaning close. "She might get lonely since she's never been alone before."

Jesse grinned, giving the little girl another kiss. "You bet, darlin'. I'll keep your mama company this morning. And I promise we'll both be here waiting when you get off the bus after school." He drew back. "Remember, you promised to draw me a picture."

Riley grinned. "I'll draw you a picture of Snoofus." She hugged the dog tighter as the bus chugged and belched to a stop just a few feet away.

"Give Mama a kiss," Hannah said, reaching for her daughter, feeling as if her heart was breaking. Riley suddenly looked so small, so fragile, so vulnerable, it only sent another round of panic through her.

Forcing it down, Hannah held Riley close to her for a moment, then kissed her cheek, drawing back with a shaky smile. ''Come on, Mama will help you onto the bus.''

Holding her child's hand, and with her own knees shaking, Hannah led the way to the open bus doors, greeting the cheerful driver and helping Riley up the large steps, watching as her daughter, dog clutched in her arms, found an empty seat and sat down.

''She's gonna be fine, darlin',''  Jesse assured Hannah, slipping an arm around her waist and pulling her close. ''Just fine.''

''I know,'' Hannah said with a sniffle, lifting a hand to wave goodbye to Riley as she gave in and leaned against Jesse, accepting his comfort. As a single mother, she couldn't remember when she'd ever had the support or comfort of someone else, especially a man. At least not when it came to her daughter. She realized it was a wonderful feeling to have someone with whom to share both her fears and her feelings.

''I feel as if I'm losing an arm.'' Hannah chewed her lip as the bus pulled away. Riley had her nose pressed against the window, a smile on her face, Snoofus clutched in her arm as she waved goodbye to them.

Jesse chuckled, slipping his other arm around Hannah and drawing her close to him. ''I know, darlin'. That's the way all mothers feel when their first goes off to school.'' Chuckling, he glanced down at her, saw her trying to blink back tears. ''My mama cried when I left for college.''

She nodded, swiping against her tears, then giving in to the need for comfort and laying her head on his chest. She could hear the familiar, rhythmic beating of his heart.

''It's all right, darlin', you might as well let it go.'' He pressed a kiss to the top of her head. ''No sense holding all that in.''

It was as if a dam had burst. Great wracking sobs began to shake her slender body. Hannah knew she was being silly, but she'd spent every waking moment of the past five years of her life with her precious daughter. Now she had to simply hand Riley over to strangers and let her make her own way in the world.

It wasn't fair, she thought with a sniffle, feeling the warmth of Jesse's hand on her back as he stroked and comforted her. The past five years had gone by so fast. It seemed like just yesterday Riley was a baby, a toddler, learning to walk, to talk, to climb up on a chair by herself. Now she'd just climbed onto a bus and left by herself.

''She really is gonna be fine, darlin', I promise,'' Jesse whispered, holding her shaking body closer. He could feel the warmth of her pressed against him, increasing that drumbeat of awareness, arousal that always seemed to awaken whenever she was near. ''She's gonna be just fine, Mama,'' he teased, drawing back to look at her and wiping away a stray tear with his thumb.

Embarrassed, Hannah glanced away. ''I'm sorry, Jesse, I know it must seem silly.''

''Not at all, darlin'. She's your baby, the most important thing in your life. Of course you're going to worry about her, especially with each new step she takes. Whether it's going off to school for the first time, or going on her first date—''

''Jesse, please.'' She laid a shaky hand to his heart and shook her head. ''I've had enough trauma for one morning.'' She glanced up to find him smiling down at her. His mouth was so close, she caught her breath, remembering the taste of that mouth. A shiver of need, desire, rolled over her, and Hannah glanced down, afraid he might be able to see everything she was feeling. ''I can't even think about her dating yet. Maybe when she's...oh, I don't know, forty or so, I'll be able to handle it, but not until then.''

He chuckled softly, nuzzling his chin across the top of her head, perfectly content to stand there at the curb with his arms around her, holding her close all morning.

''Thanks for coming this morning, Jesse.'' She lifted her head, praying he wouldn't see what she was feeling. ''I really appreciate it.'' She forced a smile. ''I don't know if I could have gotten through it alone.'' At the moment, the thought seemed incomprehensible to her. Jesse had become such an important part of their lives that having him here sharing this with her seemed perfectly normal and natural.

''You're welcome, darlin'.'' He pressed another kiss to her head. ''I wouldn't have missed it for the world.''

For the first time she remembered something. ''Jesse, why on earth do you have a ladder and all that other paraphernalia in your car?''

Keeping his arm around her, he began walking them back toward the house. ''Well, darlin', it seems to me that this old house could use a bit of sprucing up.''

Hannah came to a halt. ''Jesse,'' she began carefully, ''I know the house is in pretty dire straits, but it's going to have to stay that way for a while.'' She lifted her chin stubbornly, refusing to be embarrassed. ''At least until I get the funds to make some repairs.''

''Funds aren't what's needed here, darlin',''  he assured her with a grin. Sliding his arm free of her, he moved toward the SUV he'd been using since he'd arrived. ''Men and hands are.'' After untying the long extension ladder he'd brought, he leaned it against the vehicle and turned to flash Hannah a quick grin. ''And I've got those covered as well.''

Frowning in concern, Hannah watched him open the back door and begin extracting cans of paint, brushes and an assortment of tools she couldn't identify, let alone pronounce.

''Jesse, wait.'' She laid a hand on his back. ''I can't let you do this. I can't afford to pay for any of this stuff, nor can I pay you for your time.''

He straightened slowly, a look of hurt on his face. *''Pay me?''* he repeated softly, and she instinctively knew she'd hurt his feelings. For the life of her she didn't know how. ''Is that what you think I'm doing?'' Jesse frowned. ''Trying to earn a few bucks?''

''No, Jesse, of course not. That's not what I meant at all. Truly.'' She shrugged, wringing her hands together. ''It's just that my budget's so tight and manpower and paint cost money—''

''Tommy donated the paint, Hannah. It's been sitting

in one of the storage sheds out at the ranch for a couple of years. He figured we might as well put it to good use before it goes to waste.'' He shrugged his shoulders. ''And as for the manpower, Jared, Josh and Jake are all going to pitch in. They're coming over here this afternoon.'' He smiled as he said it, still remembering how he felt when they'd offered their help. He glanced up at the house. ''With the four of us pitching in, we should have this lovely old place back in shape in no time.''

''Jesse...'' She hesitated. ''I don't know what to say.''

''Thank you will do me fine, darlin','' he said quietly.

''Thank you, Jesse,'' she said, laying a hand to his cheek, so moved by everything he did. He never failed to surprise her. ''But there must be something I can do. I can't just stand here and watch.'' She shrugged. ''I have the day off because of Riley's first day of school.''

''Kiss me.''

Stunned, she blinked up at him, shielding her eyes against the morning sun. ''W-what?''

He chuckled at the look on her face. ''You said there must be something you can do. There is. Kiss me.''

She swallowed hard. ''Jesse, are you teasing me?''

''No, darlin', I certainly am not. You want to do something, that's what you can do.''

''Kiss you?'' She couldn't prevent her voice from edging upward in a slight squeak. ''Right here?'' she asked, backing toward the sheltered protection of the covered back porch.

With a grin, he nodded, following.

She wrung her hands together one last time. "O-okay." With her knees shaking, she stepped closer, fully intending to give him a chaste kiss on the cheek.

He didn't give her a chance. He slid an arm around her waist and hauled her into his arms. Her body almost slammed into his, and she felt the world tilt under her feet as Jesse covered her mouth with his.

This time there was no gentleness, no finesse, it was all heat, fire, desire and need.

With a moan, she stood on tiptoe, wrapping her arms tightly around his neck, drawing him closer, feeling as if she was drowning in his taste, his scent, his touch.

Jesse felt the kick of desire slam into him, dizzying him. He'd tried to keep a rein on his emotions, his desires, knowing that things were so emotionally confused he could very easily slip up, make a mistake, hurt someone.

Something he never, ever wanted to do.

But even with all the emotions swirling around and through him, the one emotion, the one need that was clear as crystal was his desire, his need for Hannah.

For the touch of her, the taste of her. He couldn't seem to get enough. The more time he spent with her, the more his fingers, his hands, his body itched to be with her, on her, in her.

The thought of lying naked with her under him, their bodies joining together in the rhythmic dance of love, caused a flash fire to spread through him, causing his body to ache and harden with need. Pressing need.

When she tangled her fingers through his hair and uttered a soft, low, sexy moan, he hauled her closer, off her feet, pressing her softness against his hardness, trying to ease the ache, knowing it would take much more than one kiss.

His hand slowly drifted from her waist, cupping her breast beneath the thin cotton of the blouse she wore. She was naked beneath, and he groaned as his fingers brushed against her nipples, already hardened, pouting for attention.

She arched against him, into his hand, whimpering his name over and over, softly, like a mantra to his ears. He deepened the kiss, slid his hand down to her waist again, then around to cup the sensuous curve of her buttocks, rubbing his hand over and over, before pulling her close so that her softness, the very essence of her womanhood was pressed against his hardness.

He was going to explode. He was almost certain of it. The warnings in his mind went off, wildly clanging, trying to get his attention, but he ignored them, knowing that he wasn't interested in anything right now except the woman in his arms.

''Jesse.'' She whispered his name against his lips as she drew back a bit so that their lips separated. Their eyes met and she groaned, diving back in, pressing her open mouth firmly against his, accepting the touch of his tongue, warm and sweet as it invaded her mouth, sending a river of shivers racing over her.

''We...shouldn't...be doing...this.'' Breathless, Hannah struggled for composure and forced herself to take a step back. Her legs were so shaky she almost keeled over.

''Can you give me one perfectly good reason why we shouldn't?'' Jesse asked, still shaken himself. He blew out a breath, then dragged a hand through his hair, surprised to find it shaking. Nothing in the world had ever felt so right as having Hannah in his arms.

"Jesse." She hesitated. She knew there were lots of reasons why they shouldn't have kissed, caressed. Why she shouldn't have let her feelings and emotions get so out of hand where he was concerned. But at the moment, she couldn't think of one. "There're a million reasons," she repeated.

"Darlin', you don't sound very sure." He grinned, then ran a finger down her nose, fearing if he did anything more he'd toss her into the backseat of his car, and privacy or propriety be damned.

"No, Jesse, I—" They jumped apart as a car skidded to a halt at the curb.

"Hannah!" Josh called, jumping out of his car. Startled, they both turned to look at him.

"What's wrong?" Jesse asked immediately, walking toward his brother and laying a comforting hand on his shoulder. Josh looked six shades of white. None of them good.

"Emma's sick. It's the flu, I think, but she can't open the diner." He turned to Hannah. "Do you think you can go over there and open the place and maybe lend a hand for a while?"

Emma, Josh's wife, owned the only diner in town. It was a popular breakfast and lunch place and closing down would not only throw the town into a tizzy and leave them nowhere to get their meals, it would also send off alarms that something was wrong with one of the Ryans.

Deliberately, Hannah stepped back and away from

Jesse, praying the heat surging through her wasn't showing on her face. "Of course, Josh." Hannah frowned. "If Emma's sick, she's going to need a cook at the diner." Her mind was already spinning ahead. "I'll go over there right now and open the place. I can stay and cook, at least until Riley comes home from school." She gave a helpless shrug. "I've got to be here to meet the bus, Josh."

"I'll meet the bus," Jesse said, "And then I'll bring Riley over to the diner and we can give you a hand as well."

"Tell you what, Jesse, bring Riley to the house. Natalie's got all the kids there, even Brie and Molly. She's afraid with Emma being sick, the kids might catch something, so she's herding them over there." He laughed. "It looks like a nursery school. Tommy's pitching in as well." He turned to Hannah. "Riley will love it. All the kids and dogs together. They'll have a ball."

She looked concerned. "If you're sure?"

"Positive. And I know Natalie won't mind." He bent and kissed Hannah's cheek in a brotherly fashion. "Thanks, Hannah, I knew I could count on you."

He turned toward Jesse. Their eyes met and held. The chasm that had separated them for so many years seemed to close in that instant, and once again they were the two youngest Ryans, close as clams, doing anything and everything for one another just as they had as children.

"Thanks, bro." Josh stepped forward, then gave Jesse a hug. For a moment, the two men clung to each other, each lost in his own memories. "I always could count on you,'' Josh said, drawing back to look at his brother.

''Hell, Josh, that's what family is for.''

Hannah stood there, her heart overflowing with joy, watching Jesse and Josh, wondering if Jesse even realized what he'd done. What he'd said.

He'd come to Josh and Emma's aid without a thought, because in Jesse's mind and heart, that's what a family did, helped each other in time of need.

Looking at Jesse and Josh, Hannah's heart filled with hope when she realized Jesse probably hadn't a clue what he'd just said; or rather, admitted, and perhaps finally, finally had accepted.

*''Hell, Josh, that's what family is for.''*

She wondered if Jesse knew it yet, but Jesse Ryan had finally, truly come home.

## *Chapter Nine*

Wiping her hands on her apron, Hannah swung through the door that led from the kitchen into the serving area of the diner, determined to have a cup of coffee. In the three and a half hours since she'd arrived and opened the diner, she hadn't sat down once.

It had been a long time since she'd stood on her feet, cooking for this many people. But now that the breakfast rush had cleared, and the diner was blissfully empty for a few moments, and she had a bit of a break before the lunch rush started, and she was determined to take a few minutes for herself. Pressing a hand to her aching back, Hannah poured herself a cup of coffee, leaning her hip against the counter.

Her face lit up when she saw Jesse walking through the door with Riley atop his shoulders.

"Sweetheart." Hannah set down her cup of coffee

and rounded the counter. ''You're home. How was your first day of school?'' Her eyes went over her daughter, inspecting every single inch of her in the way only a mother can, wanting to make sure that her child was all in one piece. Riley looked none the worse for the wear, except she had a large smudge of something sticky on her glasses, right in the middle of the left lens.

''Mama, it was so cool,'' Riley said as Jesse set her on her feet. She was clutching a large piece of construction paper in her hand.

''Cool?'' One eyebrow rose and Hannah and Jesse exchanged amused looks. ''I see you've learned a new word, sweetheart.'' Hannah reached for the piece of paper. ''Now, tell me, what's this?''

''That's for Uncle Jesse.'' She turned and grinned at him. ''It's your picture of Snoofus.''

Not trusting his voice at the moment, Jesse took the paper, pretending to examine it closely. He had to clear his throat before he spoke. ''Why, darlin', thank you. I do declare that's the prettiest picture I've ever seen.'' He turned it to show Hannah, love shining in his eyes. ''Wouldn't you agree?''

She looked at the picture carefully, grateful that Riley had already told them what it was. ''Yep, Jesse, I have to admit, that is the prettiest picture I've ever seen.''

''I made a friend, Mama. His name is Mikey,'' Riley said, scratching her nose. ''He said we could play again tomorrow. He has three brothers and no sisters. He picks his nose, but I like him.''

Hannah smothered a laugh. ''Well, sweetheart, I'm

glad you made a new friend. So I take it you liked school?''

Riley bobbed her head, eyeing the plate of doughnuts under glass on the counter.

''Are you hungry, sweetheart?'' Hannah asked with a laugh.

''Starved.'' Riley rubbed her tummy, then tried to climb up on a stool, before giving in and letting Jesse lift her. ''Could I have a doughnut?''

''No,'' Hannah said. ''But you can have some lunch. And then Uncle Jesse is going to take you to Uncle Tommy's so you can play with Timmy and Terry and the dogs for the afternoon, is that okay?''

''Yeahhhhh!'' Riley set the stool whirling and when it came to a stop, she eyed her mother dizzily. ''Are you sure I can't have a doughnut?''

''Positive.'' Hannah grinned, grateful this first day of school had come and gone. She'd made it, she thought proudly, with only a few tears and a few fears. Looking at her beautiful daughter, she could only hope that all new things in the future would be this easy.

Dusk was just settling over Saddle Falls when Jesse pulled into Hannah's driveway.

''Hannah?'' Gently, he touched her shoulder. She was so tired, she'd dozed off almost the moment she'd gotten into the car. ''We're home.''

''Home?'' She blinked up at him, lost in the moment of her dream. It had been lovely. Jesse was there. Without thinking, she lifted a hand and touched his cheek. ''You are so wonderful, Jesse,'' she murmured, pressing her mouth to his. ''Just wonderful.''

He kissed her back, nibbling at the corners of her mouth. ''Hannah-Anna, if this is the way you wake up all the time, I'm going to start mixing sleeping pills in your coffee.''

Almost fully awake now, Hannah chuckled, then pressed a hand to the back of her neck where a knot of tension had settled.

''Riley?'' she said, sitting up and glancing around. ''Jesse, we forgot to pick up Riley.''

''No, we didn't, darlin','' he said, brushing a strand of hair behind her ear. ''She's spending the night at Tommy's.'' He held up his hand the moment she opened her mouth to protest. ''Ditka's mate is about to drop her litter, and Natalie figured it might be a good learning experience for the kids. So, she's turned it into a sleepover party. She's making the kids hot dogs and sloppy joes, and yes, I know, Riley has to go to school in the morning, but I promise I'll bring her home in plenty of time to get changed and catch the bus.'' He pressed a quick kiss to her lips, longing to linger, but aware they were sitting outside in her driveway, in full view. ''Fair enough?''

Hannah nodded, stifling a yawn. ''Okay.'' She was far too exhausted to argue with him or anyone.

''Besides, you've had one helluva day.'' He smiled, cupping her chin, letting his gaze linger on her mouth again, feeling need rise like a tide, swamping him with desire. ''I thought you could use some downtime. A night off, if you will.'' His gaze studied hers. ''You hungry?''

''Starved,'' she said, pressing a hand to her tummy.

She turned to him. "I'll throw something together for us, Jesse."

"No, you won't," he corrected. "You've been cooking all day. I think I can handle dinner."

"You can cook?" she said in surprise.

"No," he laughed. "But I can do carryout. What's your pleasure? Pizza or Chinese food?"

She couldn't help but grin. "I'm so hungry, how about both?"

He laughed. "You've got a deal, darlin'."

"Full?" Jesse asked lazily as he glanced at Hannah who was sitting on the floor next to him, leaning against the couch with legs outstretched in front of her.

"Stuffed," she admitted, stifling a yawn as she glanced at him. "How about you?"

Patting his stomach, he groaned. "Stuffed as well. Although it wasn't as good as your home cooking. I reckon I'll need to climb on a treadmill if this keeps up. Your fabulous cooking must have added five pounds since I got here," Jesse said, patting his stomach.

Hannah laughed. "Jesse, you don't have an ounce of fat on you." It was true, she realized. He was an incredible specimen of a man. Tall. Lean. Slender-hipped and long-legged. The kind of man any woman would drool over, she thought in amusement. Including a woman who thought herself far too practical to be susceptible to a man's charms. But in the time since Jesse had been home, he'd proven her wrong.

"You think my cooking is fabulous?" she asked with a grin.

"Fishing for compliments?" he inquired with a smile and a lift of his eyebrow.

"Absolutely," she said with a saucy grin. " A woman never tires of compliments."

"And I reckon you haven't had all that many, have you, darlin'?"

Taken aback by the seriousness of his tone, Hannah glanced down, pretending to press a wrinkle out of her shorts. "I'm not complaining, Jesse."

"I know that, darlin'." He smiled, reaching out to cup her chin. "But then you never do." His gaze met hers and she let out a little sigh of yearning. Being this close to him was wreaking havoc with her senses. And her common sense.

"I'd better clean up," she said, preparing to stand up. He dropped an arm around her shoulder, stopping her.

"It'll wait, darlin'. Sit with me a minute and I'll help you later." He studied her face, letting his gaze lovingly roam over her eyes, her nose, that incredible, beautiful mouth. Dark had descended, but they hadn't turned on any lights. Instead, Hannah had lit an assortment of candles, which cast a soft, hazy glow across the room. "Do you know this is the first time we've ever been alone together."

She nodded. The same thing had occurred to her just moments before. Perhaps that's why she was so nervous.

"I know." She couldn't look at him, fearing he'd see the desire in her eyes.

"Is that why you're so nervous?" he asked softly, bending to nuzzle her neck. Her scent was strong here, sweet and enticing. Against his lips, he could feel her pulse scramble.

"I'm...I'm...not..." She had to swallow. It was difficult when his lips were against her skin, warming it, teasing it, making butterflies take flight in her belly. "Nervous," she finally managed to get out, making him laugh.

"Now Hannah-Anna," he whispered, tumbling her across his lap and grinning at the look on her face. "Don't you know you're not supposed to fib?"

"You sound like Riley," she complained, trying to force herself to relax as she looked up at him.

"Do I?" He bent and brushed his mouth gently, lightly, over hers in a teasing motion that had her groaning, reaching for him, winding her arms around his neck.

"Jesse." It was all she could say. His name. Half plea, half prayer as he pulled her closer until they were pressed against one another, his mouth, desperate and needy, clinging to hers, taking them deeper and deeper into the dark abyss of desire where reason fled and only feelings remained.

Panic settled in her mind, her heart, but Hannah knew without a doubt nothing had ever felt so right. So perfect.

"Jesse," she whispered again, arching against him, letting him take the kiss deeper, to a place where desire licked at her sanity, wiping away any thoughts other than the thought of how wonderful it felt to touch him.

To be touched. It had been so long, Hannah thought. So very long.

With a quick motion of his arms, he had her lying

full atop him, his arms anchored around her, holding her in place as his mouth plundered, driving her wild as desire, edgy and fierce, ripped along her nerve endings, causing soft little whimpers to escape.

"You are so beautiful," he whispered, drawing back to cup her face in her hands. "Hannah-Anna," he whispered, pressing a light kiss to her bare neck, making her shudder atop him. "So beautiful, my Hannah-Anna."

She wanted nothing more than to be beautiful for him. To be everything he wanted, needed. But she'd had so little experience with men. So little experience at this. The last time she'd been a teenager and hadn't appreciated how wonderful, how perfect such a meeting, a mating of two bodies, two souls could be.

With Jesse, she knew what was possible. And it thrilled her as nothing before.

His lips slid from her neck, to her collarbone, as his hands slowly pushed her blouse off her shoulders. Gently, reverently, he pressed a kiss to each. First one, then the other, causing a soft sigh to escape her.

He turned, flipping her onto her back beneath him, leaning up on his elbow so he could see her face in the flickering candlelight. He bent and kissed her eyelids, her nose, her mouth, teasing it until she was moaning softly again, clinging to him. His hands ached to touch her, to feel her skin against his.

Slowly, he unbuttoned her blouse, carefully spreading the material so that the pale golden skin beneath beckoned. He bent and kissed the flat of her belly, letting his tongue circle the small indentation of her belly button. Then let his mouth move upward, nuzzling, tasting, leaving a wicked wet path of desire as his tongue slid upward until it found the hard nub of her nipple. His mouth closed over it, greedily, hungrily, and she cried out, arching against him, her fingers tangling through the strands of his hair.

He suckled gently, laving the tightened bud until her body was arching to meet his, to put out the flames of desire that were flaring brightly out of control.

The locks and bolts that he'd kept on his emotions all these years seemed to come tumbling open and desire slammed into Jesse, knocking him senseless until he couldn't think, couldn't reason—only feel.

Desires so long denied demanded to be fed, and he feasted on her, unable to get enough. Certain he would go mad if he didn't fill her and this unbearable need for her he'd harbored inside.

With a quick flick of his wrist, he snapped open her shorts, pushed them down, kissing a path down the bare expanse of her thighs, making her sigh and groan, as he replaced his lips with his tongue.

''Jesse.'' Unable to bear not feeling his skin next to hers, Hannah tore at his shirt, sending his buttons flying. She leaned up, pushing the material away, kissing every inch of exposed skin she could reach, wanting, needing more.

He groaned when she reached for his zipper, twisting to help her free him from the constraint. With a groan of desire pent up too long, Jesse held her face in his hand, let his lips trail over hers as he lifted himself up, then carefully, slowly, entered her.

''Ahhh, Hannah,'' he whispered on a low moan. Everything inside him seemed to still and explode at the same time. So many feelings burst through, it was like a kaleidoscopic rainbow after a long drought, brilliant colors, different shades, streaks of feelings. He began to move, slowly at first, then faster as her legs wound around him, clinging, urging him on.

She couldn't seem to get enough of him. It simply wasn't enough. It had been so long, and yet she knew it had never, ever been like this. Where her heart felt as if it were melting, melding with his. Where her blood felt as if it were too hot for her veins. She was spiraling higher and higher, feeling, tasting, experiencing things she'd never known existed, never would forget.

"Jesse..." She couldn't stop saying his name, a fervent whisper against his neck as she clung to him, her body rising and falling with his, faster and faster until she was certain she was going to fall right off the earth.

"Hannah-Anna..." He whispered her name like a mantra over and over, then he lifted his head for one long moment and plunged into her. Plunging them both over the other edge into ecstasy.

Jesse was more than a little shaken as he looked at Hannah, who had her eyes closed and was dozing cozily in his arms. The candles had burned low, reflecting just a hint of shadows and light in the night's darkness. He couldn't stop staring at her. She was the most beautiful thing in the world. He was absolutely certain of it.

Just as certain that he was more scared than he'd ever been in his life.

Leaning up on his elbow, Jesse glanced around.

Their clothes were scattered on the living-room floor. He felt a moment of embarrassment. She deserved to have candles and flowers and satin sheets and flutes of champagne.

She deserved everything in the world.

But he wasn't certain he could give her anything.

Especially himself, he thought with another little sigh.

He didn't know if he had anything to give.

To her. To the Ryans. To anyone.

Dragging a hand through his hair, Jesse was surprised to find it shaking. He'd promised himself he'd stay emotionally detached; uninvolved until he sorted out his emotions, sorted out his memories and had time to figure things out.

He glanced at Hannah again. How on earth could he sort anything out when all he could do was think about her? And how much he wanted—needed—her?

He'd kept a lid on his emotions, holding everyone at bay for so long that now that he'd let someone close he was terrified.

Not so much for himself. But for her

He reached down and with a finger gently brushed a hair away from her closed eyes. She deserved a man who was permanent, a husband who'd give her all that she wanted, needed and deserved. And a man who could be a father to Riley, a real father, one who could love and accept her openly with no hesitation.

A man who knew who he was.

Jesse shook his head. How could he give her or Riley any part of himself when he still didn't know who he was?

He couldn't he realized.

He simply couldn't.

It wouldn't be fair to them. They deserved better.

And he knew it.

He knew he couldn't give anything to anyone until he found out for sure who he was. Jesse glanced around. And he knew he couldn't do it here. Not with her. And not in Saddle Falls. There was just too much emotional carnage here for him to sort things out. He needed time and he needed distance.

He needed Texas, he realized, pressing a gentle kiss to Hannah's forehead. What he needed was to go… home.

## *Chapter Ten*

"You're leaving, son?" Tommy asked, coming into the kitchen. He'd passed Jesse's room on his way downstairs and noted that it was empty. Devoid of any trace of the lad. Jesse's car, parked in the driveway, was loaded up with his personal belongings and looked ready to go.

Standing at the kitchen window, staring out at the Ryan land, which stretched as far as the eye could see, Jesse slowly turned and looked at his grandfather. "I think it's time, Tommy," he said softly. "I…I…need some time to think." He dragged a hand through his hair. "Some time to put things in perspective and sort them out. And I've always thought better alone."

"Aye," Tommy said, trying to hide his sadness. "I understand, son. Sometimes when something is troubling us a little solitude helps us see the way." Tommy hesitated, then stepped closer to his grandson. "You know, lad, you're always welcome here. To stay. To live. To visit. Whatever it is you find of comfort, whatever you need, we'll understand."

Jesse looked at his grandfather. "I can't tell you how much I appreciate that, Tommy." He hesitated. He hadn't realized how hard this would be. He hadn't realized that somehow when he wasn't looking, he hadn't remained quite as detached as he'd thought. "I...don't reckon I know what to say, Tommy. Goodbye...well, it just doesn't sound right." Didn't feel right either.

Tommy forced a smile. "Goodbye is such a permanent thing, don't you think? I much prefer farewell and be well." He laid a hand on his grandson's shoulder. "It says so much more, son."

Jesse nodded. He had an odd ache in his heart, an ache he couldn't ever remember having before. "I'd like to say goodbye to everyone else, if you don't mind."

"Mind?" Tommy laughed. "I'd not have it any other way, son." He met his grandson's eyes, and saw his own long-gone son, Jock, in them, and tried to hide the ache in his heart. He'd waited and prayed for the return of the lad, and he'd received his fondest wish. He'd not be ungrateful and be wishing and wanting more. He knew the lad was safe, well and a fine, proud man. What more could any man want?

"Jesse, my boy. I'm proud of you, you know that, son? Your father, may he rest in peace, would have been proud as well. He loved you, lad, more than life. As do I," Tommy added softly, swallowing hard around the lump in his throat. "Aye, son, as I do."

"Tommy..." Jesse grabbed his grandfather in a bear hug, holding him close, reveling in the security he felt there, the love that radiated from one man to the other. Jesse's throat felt thick, his voice too strained by the emotion he felt to say all the things he wanted to say, things that he suddenly realized were in his heart. He wasn't accustomed to voicing his feelings or emotions and found now he simply couldn't. "Thank you."

Tommy drew back. He'd not weep, he told himself. He'd be grateful for what little time he'd had with the lad. It was more than he'd ever expected. "You're welcome, lad." He patted Jesse's shoulder. "You're welcome. Be well, Jesse," Tommy said quietly, wiping away a tear. "Farewell."

"Jared?"

"Back here."

Jesse followed Jared's voice around the back of the henhouse where he was working on repairing some wire fencing. The moment Jared saw Jesse, he straightened.

"What's wrong?" Jared asked in alarm.

"Nothing." Jesse shielded his eyes from the early-morning sun. "I'm...leaving. I just came to say goodbye."

Jared nodded, slowly pulling off his gloves and extending his hand. "Jesse, I don't know what to say. You know you're always welcome to come back." Jared cleared his throat then glanced around the land he loved. "There's always plenty of work to do and I can always use a hand."

"I reckon I'll keep that in mind." Jesse smiled.

''Jared, would you say goodbye to Natalie and the kids for me?''

''Will do.'' Jared cocked his head, sadness in his heart. ''Think you might make your way back here again?''

Jesse grinned, fingering his Stetson. ''Say, about September?''

Jared laughed. ''How'd you know?''

''I don't know anything.'' He shrugged. ''Natalie said something about if I thought it was a zoo around here now, wait until September.''

Jared's face lit with love at the mention of his wife. Jesse realized it brought out a sense of envy in him, surprising him. He wondered what it would feel like to love someone like that. He'd never really thought about it before simply because he'd never thought such a thing possible for him before. ''Yeah, well, seems we're about to have a new addition around here. Natalie's pregnant.'' His face beamed with pride.

''Then you can bet I'll be back come September, Jared. I wouldn't want to miss the birth of my new niece or nephew.''

Jared looked at him steadily for a moment, eye to eye. ''Yeah, Jesse, the children are your nieces and nephews.''

Stunned at his own words, Jesse shifted his weight. ''Well, Jared, I've got to get going. I've got to drop Riley off at home before I take off.'' He held out his hand. ''Thanks for everything.''

Jared took his hand, then tugged Jesse close for a hug. He'd waited so long for his baby brother to come home. So many, many years. He never realized how hard it would be to let him go again. "Anytime, bro. Anytime."

With one final glance around the land that the Ryans called home, Jesse turned and started walking back toward the house.

"Jake?"

"Yeah, yeah," he grumbled, pushing open the front door of his own little house. It sat on Ryan land, within walking distance of the main house. "What the hell's so important you had to wake me up at the crack of dawn for?" Jake gave a huge yawn, then rubbed his head, squinting at the bright, harsh sunlight behind Jesse.

"I'm leaving, Jake. I came to say goodbye."

That brought Jake instantly awake. "Goodbye?" Jake frowned. "Where the hell are you going?" he growled, trying to cover his panic with anger.

"Texas," Jesse said simply. "It's time, Jake. I...I need some time to sort things out."

"Does Tommy know?" Jake asked in concern, his thoughts already on his grandfather and how he would take the news.

"Yeah, I just saw him."

"You okay?" Jake asked quietly.

Jesse shook his head. "I reckon I don't rightly know, Jake." He blew out a breath, shifting his weight, feeling an odd discomfort he couldn't identify.

"Hannah know you're leaving?" Jake didn't believe in beating around the bush. He'd seen the way Jesse looked at Hannah and vice versa.

"Not yet." Jesse glanced behind him. The back door

was still open and sunlight was pouring into the small house. "I've got to drive Riley home to get ready for school. I'll tell her then."

"Hope you're good at ducking," Jake commented, stifling a yawn. "Because I have a feeling when you tell Hannah you're leaving, she's going to be chasing you with one of her beloved frying pans."

Jesse couldn't help it. He grinned. It reminded him of the very first day he'd met Hannah. When she'd all but promised the very same thing.

Jake looked at Jesse carefully. "I've known her my whole life, bro, and I've never seen her look at a man the way she looks at you. That's not a look a man usually walks away from, unless the feeling isn't mutual."

Jesse glanced away, not sure how to respond. "It's not that," he admitted, not really sure how he felt about anything. "It's just...I need some time to sort things out."

"I understand," Jake said with a nod.

They stood there for a moment, merely taking each other's measure. Finally, Jesse spoke. "Jake, I don't know what to say." He held out his hand. Jake ignored it, dragging his brother close for a hug. After a brief moment, Jake thumped him on the back, then drew back to look at him.

"Listen to me, Jesse. You're family. And we Ryans, we stick together. You got it?" He gave his brother a poke in the chest just to be certain he got the message. "You need anything, ever, anything at all, you give a holler, you hear? I'm only a few hours away by plane.

You got it? I don't care how old or how big you are, you're still my baby brother.''

''I got it,'' Jesse said, his own emotions kicking in, clogging his throat. He'd never imagined it would be so hard to leave.

''Good.'' Jake yawned. ''Now get outta here so I can get some more shut-eye.'' He clamped a hand on Jesse's shoulder, wanting one last connection, one last contact. ''And remember what I said.'' Jake grinned. ''Duck.''

Jesse found Josh next door, at his own little house that bordered the Ryan ranch. Emma was still under the weather and in bed, and he found Josh trying to stuff some putrid orange-colored baby food into little Brie's resisting little mouth.

''Josh, morning.'' Jesse tried not to grin. Josh had more baby food on his shirt than the baby probably had in her tummy. ''Need a hand here?'' he asked just as Brie let loose a loud, wet raspberry, spreading something orange all over Josh's white shirt.

''How on earth do women feed them?'' Josh asked, grabbing the towel Jesse offered and wiping his face, his shirt, and Brie's mouth. ''For someone so little, she's like an octopus, doing sixteen different things at once.'' He reached out and grabbed the bottle that tiny fingers were reaching for. ''I don't know how Emma handles her.''

''How's Emma doing?'' Jesse asked, eyeing the baby. She was a beauty.

''Still sick as a dog,'' Josh admitted with a sigh. ''So as soon as I feed Brie, or she gets me to cry uncle, whichever comes first, I'm taking her over to Natalie.'' Josh glanced up. ''Something on your mind, Jesse?''

''I just came by to say goodbye.''

Josh merely stared at him for a moment. A million emotions fluttered through him. ''You're leaving?'' he asked quietly.

Jesse nodded. ''I think it's for the best. For now.'' Jesse fingered his Stetson. ''I need some time to sort things out. Think them through.'' He blew out a breath. ''So much has happened in such a short time, Josh, I need some time to get a handle on them.''

''Are you coming back?'' Josh asked, lifting Brie from her high chair and cradling her in his lap. The need to hold something right now was strong.

''Don't reckon I know yet, Josh.'' Jesse grinned. ''Guess that's one of the things I need to find out.''

''I understand,'' Josh said, not understanding anything of the kind. ''I hope you know how much it's meant to us—all of us—to have you here, Jesse, I'm just sorry you're leaving.''

Jesse smiled, running a finger over the baby's cheek. It was as soft as down. ''Thanks, Josh.''

''And hey, don't worry about Hannah's house. Jake, Jared and me, we'll take care of it. A few weekends and it'll be looking like new.''

Just like that, they stepped into the breach and picked up the slack. His brothers. His eyes were stinging and when he met Josh's gaze, he felt his heart ache again. ''Thanks, Josh. I appreciate it.'' He shifted his weight uncomfortably. ''Well…I'd better shove off. I've got a long way to go.''

Josh stood up. ''Take care of yourself, Jesse,'' he said quietly.

''I will.'' Jesse extended his hand. Josh took it and for a moment they looked at each other, memories and feelings flowing freely from one heart to the other.

''You take care of that wife of yours.'' Jesse bent and kissed Brie on the cheek. ''And this little lady as well.'' His voice was shakier than he would have liked.

''I will, Jesse. I will.'' Josh hesitated, then started walking Jesse toward the door. ''You take care of yourself.'' Jesse turned, and he and Josh hugged. Jesse closed his eyes, wondering why he felt so...lost. So adrift. He hadn't had that feeling in quite a while, not since before he'd arrived, but now it was back. And he didn't like it.

''Take care, bro. Call if you need anything.'' Josh stood in the doorway, watching his brother leave, with a deep-seated fear that he'd never see him again.

''Hi, Mama,'' Riley called as she dashed into the house. ''I got to get dressed for school. Uncle Jesse brought me home and the dog had puppies. I picked out a girl puppy, is that okay, Mama? I'm gonna call her Miss Muff'n Stuff, is that okay?''

Before Hannah had a chance to answer, Riley was racing through the kitchen, and up the stairs to change.

''Good morning,'' Hannah said to Jesse, who stood in the doorway looking a tad uncomfortable. She reached up on tiptoe to kiss him. ''I'm sorry I fell asleep last night.'' She couldn't help the smile that filled her face, her heart. ''And thanks for your note. I found it when I woke up this morning.''

In spite of the promise he'd made to himself, he reached out and laid a hand to her cheek. "Don't be sorry, darlin', about falling asleep. You were exhausted." He shrugged. "It's understandable."

"Thank you, Jesse," she said a bit shyly. "For last night." Her eyes slid closed in memory for a moment and then she sighed. "It was…wonderful."

"That it was, darlin'." Unable to resist, he drew her close and kissed her, wanting to hold her close just once more. Her arms instinctively went around him and he could feel her soft, feminine curves pressing against him, making him ache with remembrance and need. With deliberate effort, he drew back as Riley bounced back down the stairs.

"Am I late, Mama?" she asked, rushing into the kitchen and turning this way and that looking for her things.

"No, sweetheart." Hannah glanced at the kitchen clock. "You've still got a few minutes." Hannah grabbed Riley's snack off the counter. "Put this in your bookbag, honey."

"It's for recess, right?" Riley asked with a grin. "I'm gonna share with Mikey today." She struggled to get the straps of her bookbag all the way up her shoulders. Instinctively, Jesse reached out and helped her.

"Hannah, do you mind if I walk Riley to the bus? I'd like to talk to her."

Hannah looked at him carefully. Something was wrong, she could see it in his eyes and by the way he was standing. It sent a chill racing over her.

"Sure, Jesse. Go ahead." As she watched him take

Riley's hand, and lead her out the door and down the walk, Hannah couldn't help but feel a premonition of fear.

Something was wrong.

She knew it as surely as she knew her own name.

Hannah's gaze shifted to the window and she noticed Jesse's car. Then she saw the luggage in the back seat and she pressed trembling hands to her lips.

Oh God.

He was leaving.

"You're leaving, aren't you?" she said the moment he'd put Riley on the bus and walked back in the house. Biting back tears, Hannah clenched her hands together so he wouldn't see them trembling.

"Yes, darlin', I'm afraid I am." He shifted, then reached out to touch her, but she drew back, away from him, unable to bear the thought that he could walk away from her after last night, after what they'd shared and could have together. It hurt far worse than she'd ever imagined.

"Why?" she demanded. "Why are you leaving?"

He shook his head. "You knew all along I was leaving, darlin'. I never tried to hide it from you." He wondered if he looked as miserable as he felt.

"But what about Tommy? Your brothers?" Her voice caught and she struggled for control, trying not to let the fear and panic have free rein. "Are you simply going to turn your back on your family and walk away from them?"

Was he simply going to turn his back on her and walk away?

How could he? she wondered.

Especially after last night.

After what they'd shared.

Fighting back tears, Hannah clenched her fists until her nails bit into her palms. She knew better, knew she should have never allowed herself to let him get close to her or to her daughter. Knew she had no business not guarding her heart from him. She knew better and had let it happen anyway.

She had no one to blame but herself for this horrendous pain tearing through her.

''Darlin', that's what I'm trying to tell you. I'm not turning my back on anyone.'' He stepped closer, would have pulled her into his arms if he didn't see the coldness and pain in her eyes. He'd promised her she'd always be safe with him. And he'd broken that promise to her. Guilt washed over him and Jesse knew there was no way he could make this up to her.

Hannah was hurt.

And he felt like an absolute heel.

''Not turning your back?'' she cried, fear and pain mingling. ''Not walking away? Then what do you call it, Jesse?'' she asked, her voice rising. She took a step closer and the look on her face had him taking a step back, remembering Jake's warning. ''Just what exactly do you call it?''

He was turning his back on her just as another man had once done. He'd won her heart, and now he was simply going to walk away from her as if her heart, her life and her feelings were of no consequence.

Another thought had a pain searing through her. ''Tommy. Oh my God, does Tommy know?'' Now tears began in earnest. She couldn't bear the thought of Tommy being hurt, not by Jesse, not after all these years of waiting and longing.

''Yes, darlin'. Everyone knows—except for Riley,'' he added softly, making her eyes widen.

''Look, darlin', I'm sorry, truly I am. I never meant to hurt you.'' How could he tell her what he was feeling when he didn't understand it himself? Didn't understand the confusing mix of feelings and emotions that had been dogging him for months, making him doubt everything he ever believed about himself and his life.

How could he tell her he couldn't offer himself to her, to Riley, to anyone until he knew exactly *who he was.*

*And where he belonged.*

Looking at the pain and sadness on Hannah's face, Jesse knew he couldn't tell her any of that, not without hurting her further.

''I'm sorry, Hannah-Anna,'' he said softly, lifting a hand to her cheek for one last moment, before she turned away. ''I'm truly sorry.''

She gave her head an angry toss. ''And just what are you sorry for, Jesse?'' Her eyes blazed at him, making the ache inside him sharper. ''Sorry for turning your back on your own family? Or are you sorry for turning your back on me?'' She hadn't meant to say that, hadn't meant for him to know what was in her heart, fearing it would frighten him. Now it really didn't seem to matter.

''I'm sorry for all of it, darlin','' Jesse said slowly,

settling his Stetson on his head. "I'm just plain... sorry."

She nodded, crossing her arms across her chest as if she could hold all the pain in. "Fine, you're sorry." She merely glared at him, knowing if he didn't leave soon he was going to have to watch her fall apart right in front of his eyes. "If you're leaving, then leave, Jesse." They were the hardest words she'd ever had to say. "I've got work to do."

He nodded, then turned, pausing to look back at her, his eyes filled with an emotion she couldn't identify. "Hannah-Anna," he whispered, reaching out a hand toward her. "You'll tell Riley for me?"

Nodding, she stepped back, and couldn't stop the tears from filling her eyes.

"Yes, Jesse," she whispered, her voice cracking. "Please...just...go."

Covering her tear-stained face with her hands so he wouldn't witness her pain, Hannah didn't open her eyes again until she heard the door shut quietly behind him.

Jesse decided to drive back to Texas, rather than take a plane, because he needed some time to think, to absorb everything that had happened to him.

With every passing mile, the ache in his heart grew stronger, bolder, and his mind, his memories, became clearer, closer.

These past few months he'd been searching for Jesse Ryan, searching for the boy who'd been stolen so many years ago.

All these months, he'd been wondering who he was and where he belonged. But as he drove Jesse realized that his emotions weren't as clouded or as confused as he thought.

His whole life he'd had a hard time with emotion, had had a hard time getting close to anyone or letting them close. And he'd never understood it or questioned it. He'd merely accepted it. That's the way he was.

That's the way *Jesse Garland* was, he realized. Maybe, as Hannah had pointed out, Jesse Garland had become that way—distant, unemotional, detached—in order to protect himself so that Jesse Garland wouldn't suffer the same devastating pain that little Jesse Ryan had suffered. It had merely been a cover of protection.

The past few weeks he'd learned a little bit about who Jesse Ryan had been. Jesse Ryan had been part of a huge, loving family. A little boy who'd loved freely, openly and without fear. A little boy who'd been doted on and spoiled by his parents, his grandfather and his brothers. *Jesse Ryan had been a boy filled with hope and love.*

But somehow that little boy had been lost, and Jesse Garland had taken his place.

So who was *he* really? Jesse wondered as the miles passed and he got farther and farther away from Saddle Falls.

Jesse Garland would never have allowed himself to fall in love with Hannah. Or Riley, he thought, recognizing for the first time that the emotions he felt inside, emotions that had haunted him from the moment he'd walked out of her house were…love.

*He was in love with Hannah.* The knowledge was staggering, and for the first time in his life Jesse understood what he was feeling, what was in his heart.

He loved Hannah more than life itself, with the same kind of love and devotion he'd seen on his brothers' faces—Josh when he looked at Emma, Jake when he looked at Rebecca, and Jared when he looked at Natalie. He'd envied those looks, envied them but knew he could never have that.

*Jesse Garland* could never have that, a small voice whispered. He could never open up his emotions, allow himself to love or be loved.

But maybe *Jesse Ryan* could.

Jesse's thoughts drifted to Tommy and he couldn't prevent a smile. Tommy was the most incredible man he'd ever met. Loving and kind, and with a strong sense of himself and family.

Jesse Garland would never be able to understand someone like Tommy.

*But Jesse Ryan understood him perfectly.*

Jesse thought about his brothers, Jake, Jared and Josh. There was a connection between them, a connection that had no beginning and no end and was strong as the love that flowed through their veins, uniting them.

Jesse Garland would never be able to accept that kind of connection, that kind of closeness.

*But Jesse Ryan accepted it with ease, and in fact, relished it.*

Jesse Garland was a bleak, solitary man who harbored no hopes, no dreams for the future.

*But Jesse Ryan was a man who had hopes, dreams and wanted a future and a family. A woman of his own to love, a child of his own to care for.*

Jesse Garland would never understand the love and

commitment to the land and the way Saddle Falls was as much a part of the Ryans as the sun to morning.

*But Jesse Ryan understood it, and felt the love of the land in his hands as the rich dark earth slithered through his fingers, generation after generation.*

*Jesse Ryan understood that Saddle Falls, the small town that had grown along with the Ryan clan, was and always would be...home.*

"Damn!" Jesse hit the brakes, nearly swerving off the interstate. Ignoring the blare of horns behind him, he glanced in his rearview mirror before crossing three lanes of traffic in order to make the nearest exit.

He had to turn around.

He was going the wrong way.

He knew it now.

Knew it in his heart, knew it in his soul.

Jesse slowed and glanced in his rearview mirror. He felt a burden lift from his shoulders and he smiled, a golden beautiful smile, recognizing the face in the mirror for the first time in almost twenty years.

"Well, hello, Jesse Ryan," he said to himself. "I think it's time for you to go home."

"Now, Riley honey, please don't lose your bookbag," Hannah said, hurrying along and taking her daughter's hand as they walked toward the bus stop. "Do you have your snack for recess?"

"Yes, Mama," Riley said with a grin. "I put it in my bag. Can I share with Mikey again today?"

Hannah smiled. "Yes, honey. I even put in an extra snack for him."

"I like Mikey. He says I could be his sister."

Sister. Hannah sighed, remembering a time when she was a young girl and a little boy had told her that.

*Jesse.*

She pushed the thought away, unwilling to indulge herself any longer. He'd been gone almost twenty-four hours, and although she went through all the motions necessary to keep her life together, her heart wasn't in it, simply because her heart was broken.

"Mama?" Riley looked up at her. "You said Uncle Jesse wasn't coming back."

Hannah sniffled, then glanced down at her daughter, knowing her daughter's heart was aching as much as her own. "That's right, sweetheart," she said gently, going down so she was eye level with her. "Remember yesterday how I explained it to you?" *Tried* to explain it to Riley. How could Hannah explain something she didn't understand herself?

"But Mama, Uncle Jesse's right there." Riley pointed behind her and Hannah turned to see Jesse's SUV pull to a stop right by the driveway.

"Hi, Uncle Jesse," Riley called, bouncing on her feet and trying to tug free of her mother. Hannah held on to her daughter tightly.

"Jesse?" Hannah's heart flipped over and she blinked several times, not certain she wasn't imagining him. "Jesse?" she said again.

"It's me, darlin'," he said with a smile, shutting the truck door behind him. He was dead tired. He'd driven nonstop for almost twenty-four hours. He hadn't slept, shaved or bathed, and knew this probably wasn't his finest hour.

But he didn't care. He couldn't wait; he had to come back. He couldn't wait to get home.

Hope and anger rose in equal measures and Hannah wasn't certain what to do as he walked toward her, his gaze never leaving hers.

"Are you all right?" Hannah asked, letting her shocked gaze take him in. "You…look…terrible."

He laughed, scooping Riley up in his arms, needing to hold her. "Yep, I reckon that's a fact."

"I missed you, Uncle Jesse," Riley said, giving him a sloppy kiss on the cheek. "Lots and lots."

"You did, darlin'?" Jesse drew back to look at her. Lord, how he loved this little imp. "Well, darlin', I missed you, too." He pressed his forehead to hers and let a sigh of relief free. "Lots and lots as well."

"Did you miss Mama, too?"

Jesse's gaze slid to Hannah's. She stood still, staring at him with hope in her heart, in her eyes. Seeing him holding her daughter in his arms was almost too much for her to bear.

"I reckon I missed your mama lots and lots, too, darlin'." He paused. "That's why I came home."

*Home.* Hannah heard the word, the word she'd waited and yearned and longed to hear from him. *Home.* Jesse was home. Hope flared like a beacon inside her heart.

"Are you gonna stay, Uncle Jesse? Are you?"

He laughed. "Well, darlin', do you and your mama want me to stay?"

"Yes, yes!" Riley cried, winding her arms around his neck. "We want you to stay, don't we, Mama?"

Hannah's hand went to her throat where her heart

seemed to have lodged. ''Jesse?'' She couldn't get the words out. ''What...what are you saying?'' She shook her head, afraid to hope, afraid to have her heart broken all over again. ''What are you doing here?''

He glanced around then shrugged. ''This is my home, Hannah-Anna,'' he said quietly, slowly walking toward her. ''My home.''

Her heart began to thud in reckless, wild hope. ''Home, Jesse? You mean Saddle Falls?''

He grinned, reaching out a hand to take hers. ''Saddle Falls, Tommy, my brothers.'' His gaze met hers, strong, steady. ''You and Riley. This is my home, Hannah-Anna.'' He glanced around, savoring the connection just touching her produced. ''This is where I belong.'' He kissed Riley's cheek. ''I know that now.'' He chuckled in embarrassment. ''Maybe it took me a while to figure it all out, but—''

''But what about Jesse Garland?'' She had to know, had to ask, afraid of being hurt again. ''What about Texas? Your ranch?''

He shook his head, then smiled, feeling comfortable in his skin for the first time in a long, long while. ''Well, darlin', funny thing about that. Texas to me is just a state now. As for the ranch, I'm going to sell it, I never belonged there. Jesse Garland is just someone I once knew a long time ago.'' He shrugged. ''Doesn't make a heckuva lot of sense, maybe, but that's the only way I can explain it.'' He held her hand tighter. ''I know who I am, Hannah, and I know where I belong. I'm Jesse Ryan, and I belong here, in Saddle Falls, with Tommy, my family, and especially with you and Riley. I love you,'' he said, growing alarmed when her eyes filled. "Good Lord, darlin', don't cry." He brushed the tears from her cheeks. "I don't know what to do with a woman who's crying." He dug into his pocket for a handkerchief, then shoved it at her. "Here, darlin', please don't cry."

"I love you, too, Jesse," Hannah said with a laugh, surprised to see him so unglued by something as simple as tears. She took a step closer, needing to touch him. Laying a hand to his chest where she could feel his heart beat, she glanced up at him. "I love you so much, Jesse Ryan."

"I love you, too, Uncle Jesse."

"You do, darlin?" He looked at Riley. "Well, I love you, too, but I was wondering, how would you feel about calling me Daddy instead of Uncle Jesse?"

Riley's eyes widened into saucers. "You're gonna be my daddy?"

Jesse turned to Hannah. "If your mama says it's okay, I'd sure like to be, darlin'."

"Mama?" Riley turned to her mom, excitement in her eyes. "Is it okay? Pul-lease? Could Uncle Jesse be my daddy?" She turned back to Jesse. "Are you gonna be a real daddy like Uncle Josh and Uncle Jared and Uncle Jake?"

"Just like them, darlin'," he said, pressing his face into the silk of her hair and holding her close.

"Could I have a baby brother or sister then?" Riley asked, making Jesse throw back his head and laugh.

"Well, darlin', I do believe we'd better talk to your mama about that?" His gaze found hers. "What do you say, Hannah-Anna? Think you're ready to give motherhood another whirl?" He grinned. "I mean, we've got a ways to go to catch up with the rest of the family, but I think with practice we can do a fine job of it.''

''You mean keep up our end of the Ryan clan?'' She beamed at him, loving him, wanting only to be with him. And have his children. Their children.

''That's about right, darlin'.'' He hesitated, frightened for the first time since he'd turned the car around. ''So what do you say, Hannah-Anna?'' He waited, his heart in his mouth.

She went up on tiptoe and pressed her lips to his. ''I love you, and yes, I'll marry you and have babies with you.'' She laughed as Riley let loose a cheer. ''Lots of babies,'' she added with another kiss. Her heart was full to bursting as she looked at her precious daughter, whom she loved more than life itself. Then shifted to the man she loved just as much. Her family, Hannah thought, finally. It was everything she'd always wanted, dreamed of, yearned for. And now, because of Jesse, she had it all. With tears in her eyes, she pressed another kiss to his lips. ''Welcome home, Jesse.'' Her voice caught and she had to cling to him. ''Welcome home.''

# *Epilogue*

"Can I come in, lassies?" Tommy knocked on the bedroom door gently, smiling at the cluster of voices and laughter within.

"Come on in, Grandpop," Riley said, pulling open the door with a smile. Dressed in a floor-length dress of pale rose and matching shoes, she looked like a miniature flower in bloom.

Now that Jesse was marrying her mama, Tommy was her grandpop, just like Terry, Timmy, Brie, Molly, and J.J. and Joey. And she just loved saying it. Grandpop. She'd always wanted a daddy and a grandpop, and now she had both.

With a grin, Tommy surveyed the room. Natalie, Emma and Rebecca were all dressed in identical rose dresses and were helping Hannah with her wedding dress. The sight of all his granddaughters-in-law brought a tear to his eye.

"Lassies, you all look lovely. Just lovely." One by one he went to them and kissed them on the cheek, stopping with Hannah, who was resplendent in a floor-length gown of eggshell with a matching veil. "Aye, lass, a more beautiful bride I've not seen on this day." He kissed her cheek again. "Just beautiful."

"Thanks, Tommy." She grabbed his hand, held it. "And thank you for everything." She glanced around. Tommy had insisted on having a true Ryan-family wedding at the ranch. He'd invited the entire town and, from the looks of the backyard, anyone he'd ever known. "It's going to be a beautiful wedding."

"Aye," he said with a nod, leaning on his cane. "As it should be. When the youngest of the Ryan clan weds, it should be a celebration." His eyes twinkled. "Now, with any luck at all, by this time next year, we'll have a new Ryan addition to be celebrating."

Natalie, Emma and Rebecca exchanged amused glances. Natalie stepped forward, touching Tommy's arm. "Uh…Tommy, there's something we would like to tell you. We thought it appropriate today."

Tommy's gaze went from Natalie to Emma to Rebecca. "And what's that, lassies?"

"Well," Natalie began, looking at the others and trying not to smile, "it seems we're going to have a few Ryan additions *before* next year." She couldn't help but beam, placing a hand on her tummy. "Well, Tommy, it seems as if I'm expecting again."

"Again?" he said in absolute joy. "Again!" he repeated with a laugh and a clap of his cane on the floor when Natalie nodded. "Now that's what I call a fine announcement and cause for celebration." He chuckled. "There's nothing more I like than more babies."

Hannah patted his shoulder. "Uh...Tommy?"

He turned to her. "Yes, lassie?"

Hannah glanced at her sisters-in-law, then at Riley.

"Grandpop." Riley tugged on the hem of his jacket. "I'm getting a brother or sister. But it's gonna take forever, months and months and months, but she's gonna look like me. Daddy said so."

"He did now, did he, lassie?" Tommy said, unable to contain his joy, reaching for the child's hand. "Well now, isn't that grand?"

"Grand indeed," Hannah said, placing a hand on her tummy, thrilled at the life, the love growing there, knowing she'd never been happier or more content in her life.

Tommy Ryan was not a man ashamed of tears, and they came now, filling his eyes, spilling down his cheeks. "'Tis a joyous day indeed, then," he said with a sniffle, tugging a handkerchief out of his pocket and swiping at his nose. "A wedding and more babies." He shook his head. "'Tis a great day for the Ryans. Truly a great day indeed."

"We love you, Tommy," Hannah said, kissing his cheek.

"Yes, Tommy, very much." Emma, Natalie and Rebecca joined in, each in turn giving his cheek a kiss.

Still sniffling, Tommy wiped his nose again and then stuffed his handkerchief in his pocket. "Well, lassies, I best let you finish getting ready." He looked down at Riley. ''Come along with Grandpop. And I'll tell you a story about the Ryan clan.'' He led her out of the bedroom and down the stairs, pausing at the kitchen window for a moment to look out.

''I can't see, Grandpop,'' Riley complained.

''Aye, 'tis true, lassie.'' He lifted her up so they could both see out the window.

''There's Daddy,'' Riley said, pointing toward Jesse who stood right off the patio where the wedding canopy had been set up, talking to his brothers.

''Aye, it is, isn't it, lass.'' Tommy let his eyes feast on his grandsons.

Jake, Jared, Josh and Jesse. Dear Jesse.

Tommy sighed, his heart full of love and gratitude. It had been a long, lovely life, he decided. Filled with ups and downs, but more love than a man could wish for. He'd been blessed with a family only few would ever know, blessed with a strength of love and loyalty only few would ever experience.

When he'd come to America so many years ago, he'd had nothing at all but wild hopes and incredible dreams. He smiled. And it was here, on this land, in this country of so much opportunity that they'd all come true.

He'd had more than any man could wish for, more than any man deserved, and through it all he'd never forgotten the most important thing: family was everything.

His gaze went over his grandsons again, strong, loyal and, above all, men of courage and conviction. Men who knew and understood about the land, about their home, and most importantly, understood the true meaning of family.

And now, as time passed by, his grandsons would carry the mantle for the Ryan clan to another generation, teaching the next what he'd taught them. And so on and so on.

Love and family were a never ending circle, he thought, and as long as there was love, there was hope.

Looking at his grandsons, Tommy felt another swell of tears. "Dear Jock," he whispered, looking up toward the clear blue skies, where he was certain his long-gone son was watching. "You would have been proud of your boys, son. Aye, you would have been proud indeed."

* * * * *